BURN BABY BURN
A SUPERVILLAIN NOVEL

JAMES MAXEY

For Jeremy Cavin
who first said the words "pit geek" to me while we were
sitting in a Pizza Hut on Battleground Avenue.
In the midst of the mundane, wonders abound.

Also, sincere thanks to Chandon Harris for coming up with the
"Airhead" power used by the superhero Ap in this novel.

~~Teh~~ The quick brown fox jumped over a lazy dog.The quick brown fox jumped over the lazy dog.

Sonof a bitch.

I can type.

James Maxey

Chapter One
How Sunday Met Monday

Ten Years Ago

SUNDAY JIMINEZ was fifteen when she killed her first nun. She was a relatively new arrival at the Trinity Life Solutions School. Her mother had recently remarried and to say that Sunday didn't get along with her new step-so-called-father was an understatement.

Her mother's new husband had accused Sunday of being possessed by demons. Sunday had an odd . . . well, ability didn't seem the right word to describe it. "Ability" would imply that she was "able" to control what she was doing, and she couldn't. For reasons she didn't understand, sometimes she would get hot. Really hot. She wouldn't feel any different when this happened. Her usual first clues were the faint odor of scorched cotton and, if the lights were on, tiny wisps of smoke. If the lights were off, the heat would be accompanied by a soft glow, sometimes bright enough to cast shadows. Usually, it happened in her bed. When she realized what was going on, she would jump up and find her sheets covered with scorch marks ranging from light tan all the way to charcoal black patches that crumbled when she touched them.

The therapist her mother sent her to had a simple explanation. Sunday was acting out due to her stress over Phil (her mother's latest Mr. Forever True Love). She was sneaking the iron from the laundry and burning her own sheets, then claiming ignorance of how her bed had been damaged. Basically, she was flat-out accusing Sunday of lying, though she did allow that

3

perhaps Sunday was suppressing the truth from herself.

Sunday wasn't suppressing the truth. She just wasn't telling everything she knew. She didn't think it was anyone's business that the first time she'd burned her sheets, she'd just experienced her first orgasm. This had only been six months ago, when she was still fourteen. The fifteen-year-old Sunday was embarrassed by the naiveté of her younger self. She'd still been in public school back then. Franky Bodin, a boy in her class, had gotten in trouble when he called a teacher a 'jerk-off.' Sunday was stunned that the teacher had taken offense. She'd heard the term thrown about since she was in kindergarten. In the context she normally heard it, she'd thought it mean someone was, you know, extra-jerky. Like, lift-off was when a rocket shot into space. Jerk-off was when someone was such a jerk they entered a whole new orbit of jerkdom.

She went home and used her mother's computer to look up the term. What she discovered was both mortifying and tantalizing. That night, she touched herself with some of the images she'd seen bouncing in her head. She discovered a new thing that her body could do as a result. Two new things, technically, but her first orgasm, which under different circumstances might have been utterly fascinating, lost its position of importance when she realized that her bed was almost, but not quite, on fire.

In the most technical sense, the therapist was right. Sunday was burning her sheets on purpose, sort of, a little bit. Even knowing she was literally playing with fire, Sunday had continued her experiments in bodily manipulation, not for the feelings of pleasure the act generated, but for the feeling of power. When her heart rate passed a certain level, she felt a switch click deep in the center of her belly, and suddenly heat and light would seep from her pores like flaming sweat. She couldn't trigger this just by running, which only left her tired. She needed the growing internal tightness in her abdomen to trigger the effect. The feeling was both addictive and terrifying. She dared not explain the truth to anyone. She was certain she'd be swooped off to some secret government facility where she'd be locked up and forced to masturbate in front of teams of stone-faced scientists in white lab coats. They would probe her with horrible, horrible devices, long iron sensors covered with metal studs that would force their way deep into her belly to stare at the trigger of her powers with cold, mechanical eyes. The fact that she often came while the imagined probe drew near added to her sense that, just perhaps, she was a disgusting pervert as well as an inhuman mutant. When Phil first brought up the possibility of demon possession, she shouted, "I'm my own demon!"

They sent her to boarding school.

And then she killed the nun.

The nun's name was Sister Cecilia. She taught algebra, and by the time Sunday had finished her first week of classes, she'd figured Cecilia out. The woman had obviously been a stoner in her youth, a hippy-dippy flower child who'd dressed in nothing but tie-dyes until bad acid had frightened her back to the Lord. Her algebra lessons always turned into rambling anti-drug lectures. She'd go to the blackboard to solve for "X" and wind up weeping about how ten million babies a year are born without eyes because their mothers used "E." Cecilia struck Sunday as slightly amusing and mostly harmless.

On her fifth day at the school, Sunday went into the bathroom near the science lab. She smelled cigarettes. The back room was L-shaped, with a short line of sinks when you first walked in, then a long row of stalls around the corner facing windows to the courtyard. Turning the corner, she found Anjelica and Moon standing next to an open window, their hands behind their backs. Sunday had made no friends since coming to the school, but she'd noticed these two girls in English Composition. Jewelry was strictly forbidden at the Trinity Life Solutions School, but a line of holes on Anjelica's left ear indicated she'd once had a whole row of rings or studs along the upper edge. Anjelica was tall and blonde but a little heavy set. Moon was thin as a broomstick, with straight black hair and dark bags under her eyes that made her look like she hadn't slept in weeks.

"You can keep smoking," Sunday said. "I'm cool."

Anjelica and Moon relaxed. They'd already thrown their lit cigarettes out the window but Anjelica reached into her bra and produced a pack of Virginia Slim Menthol's and a pink BIC lighter.

Anjelica popped one of the cancer sticks in her mouth and handed the pack to Moon while she struggled to get the lighter going.

"Almost out of gas," she grumbled.

"Fag?" Moon asked, holding the pack toward Sunday.

"She's on a British kick," Anjelica said. "It's their word for cigarette."

Sunday was bugged that Anjelica thought she wouldn't know that, but kept quiet. She took the cigarette and popped it between her lips.

"Fucking lighter," Anjelica grumbled as the BIC continued to produce only sparks. "I don't suppose you have one, do you?"

Sunday didn't carry a lighter. But she unconsciously felt completely at ease in the company of two fellow reprobates. She lifted her right index finger to the tip of the cigarette and . . . something happened. She couldn't really explain it. Even though her heart wasn't racing, and even though she didn't feel the tightness in her gut, the tip of her finger flared like a flashbulb. In the aftermath, the cigarette was half the length it had been, but what was left was burning. She sucked in the smoke, then coughed violently. She was embarrassed to reveal she was such a novice.

Sunday glanced toward the two girls, worried they'd laugh at her incompetence as a smoker.

Instead, they were staring at her, slack-jawed. Both were pale as ghosts, their cheeks flecked with gray ash from the disintegrated cigarette.

"How did you do that?" Anjelica whispered.

"Um," said Sunday.

Such was the intensity of the moment, none of them had heard the bathroom door open. Sister Cecilia came around the corner and both Moon and Anjelica froze, staring at her.

Sunday looked over her shoulder, the cigarette still dangling on her lips.

She jumped back as the nun snatched the cigarette from her mouth.

"This is how it begins!" Sister Cecilia screamed, her spittle spraying Sunday's face. "Tobacco is the worst gateway drug! Do you want to be a whore, selling your body to disease-ridden beasts to get your next fix? Do you want to die on some filthy mattress covered in your own vomit?"

Sunday crossed her arms and turned her face away from the nun. "It's just a cigarette. Chill out."

"You, young lady, are the one who's going to chill out!" the nun shouted, grabbing Sunday by the wrist. The middle-aged woman had a grip like a gorilla.

"Let go!" Sunday protested. "You're hurting me!"

"You don't know what hurt is," Sister Cecilia said, dragging her forward.

"I said let go!" Sunday tried to pull away, but couldn't break Cecilia's grip. She grabbed hold of a stall door but felt her fingers slipping as the raging nun proved superior at tug-of-war.

Sunday wondered if she could make her wrist flash, the way she'd made her finger flash.

There was heat. There was light. In the aftermath, Sister Cecilia lay dead, her hand completely gone, her arm nothing but blackened bone all the way up to the shoulder. Her habit was on fire. Seconds later the sprinklers came on, drenching them all.

Sunday stared down at the woman she'd just killed. She suspected that a normal person who wasn't a pervert and a mutant might feel remorse at this moment. Cecilia had gotten what was coming to her. The nun had been the one to turn this into a physical confrontation.

Sunday turned and found Anjelica glued to the far wall, eyes filled with terror. Moon was sobbing in a tight fetal ball at Anjelica's feet.

The two girls would never be her friends now. All she would ever have was their fear. That gave her a little thrill, the thought of being feared.

"Tell anyone what you saw and I'll kill you," she said, her voice low and firm. She thought her words sounded especially dramatic with the fire alarms blaring, the hiss of the sprinklers overhead, and the sizzle and pop of nun-fat still burning behind her.

But inside of fifteen minutes, both girls had talked and Sunday was on her way to jail. She was placed in a holding cell by herself. She wasn't sure why she was afforded the privacy. Obviously, they couldn't put her in a holding cell with men, and maybe there just weren't that many women getting arrested at ten a.m. on a Friday. Her first thought on being left in the empty holding cell was, "Good. I can finally pee." Her trip to the bathroom at the girl's school had gone in a direction she hadn't really planned. But even though she was alone in the cell, she still couldn't go, because there was a surveillance camera in the hall aimed directly at the single exposed toilet. Did the ACLU know about this?

The thing was, she really needed to pee. She'd watched enough television to know that at some point she'd be given an attorney, but doubted she could wait until she had legal representation to argue her right to urinate in private.

The camera had to go.

In the police car, she'd tried to melt the handcuffs. She'd mentally tightened every muscle in her gut one by one to trigger the release of heat, to no avail. The problem, of course, was that her powers normally kicked in when she wasn't thinking about them. Once you start thinking about not thinking about something, it's all you can think about.

She had to try. She went to the bars of her cell and reached into the empty hallway, pointing her fingers straight at the camera. In her mind's eye, she could imagine jets of flame spouting from her fingertips and engulfing the camera. She furrowed her brow and clenched her teeth, her arm trembling as she willed the fire to come.

After fifteen minutes, her shoulder was really sore. Worse, with her arm stretched up like that, whoever was on the other side of that camera probably thought she was some kind of Nazi. She could stand people thinking she was demon-possessed, and she was resigned to the fact that word would soon spread that she was a horrible nun-burning mutant, but getting branded a Nazi was too much.

She lowered her arm and walked to the toilet. If she kept her skirt down, really, how much could they see? She reached under the hem and hooked her fingers into the edge of her panties.

Behind her, a man cleared his throat.

Sunday spun around to find a middle-aged white guy in the cell with her, leaning against the bars, his back to the camera. He had his arms crossed and he stared at her with a look that made no sense at all. It was the same look her mother had given her the first time she'd brought home a report card that was all A's. It was a look of pride.

"Are you my lawyer?" she asked, smoothing down her skirt.

"Do I look like a lawyer?" the man asked, in a tone of mock offense.

Sunday didn't know any lawyers, so it was tough to say. She'd assumed a lawyer would be wearing a suit, but maybe that was just on television. This man was wearing blue jeans and scuffed up Nikes. He wore a white cotton button-up shirt, a bit wrinkled. She guessed he was probably close to fifty, since his hair was mostly gray. He wore it long, not down to his shoulders, but still kind of shaggy. He had a deep tan and his mouth and eyes had settled into kind of a smirk. The wrinkles on his face hinted that this was a common expression for him.

She asked, "So . . . are you a cop? Because this conversation can stop now." She'd been read her rights. She liked having rights.

The man shook his head. "If you must identify me by a career, I used to be a physicist working for the army. Then, I blew up the world. Then I rebuilt it. So, I guess my job description is god."

"I thought they had a separate ward for psychos."

"Nope," said the man. He glanced around. "But they sure give nun-burners their space."

As he spoke, three female guards burst through the door at the end of the hall.

"I've been spotted," said the stranger, reaching into his back pocket. He produced a small black pistol and fired three shots toward the guards. All three dropped instantly.

"Oh my God!" Sunday screamed, the report of the pistol still ringing in her ears.

The man shrugged. "There are better places for us to have this conversation." He pulled a calculator out of his front pocket and began to punch in numbers.

Sunday felt her body fold at an unnatural angle. Before she fully understood what was happening, she found herself staring at the back of her knees.

Then her body snapped back to normal and they were standing in the middle of a vast, trackless desert. The sky above was full of stars, so crisp and clear that Sunday could see the Milky Way. She spun around, off balance in the shifting sand. She dropped to her knees, temporarily forgetting how to breathe. The sand burned like it had just been pulled straight out of an oven.

"What just happened?" she gasped.

The man held up the calculator. "I moved us to the Sahara so we could talk in peace. This is my space machine. Like it? I can move anything I wish anywhere I wish by something analogous to a cut and paste of spatial coordinates. I should have built this years ago, but I got side-tracked trying to perfect a teleportation belt."

"Who are you again?" Sunday asked.

"My original name was stolen from me," the man said. "Now, I answer to Rex Monday. It's a play on words. Get it?"

Sunday didn't get it.

"Are you with the government?" she asked. "Are you here because of my powers?"

"No," said Monday. "I'm not with the government. Yes, I'm here because of your powers, though that's just part of the reason."

"Just part?"

"I'm also your father," said Monday. "Your real father. I'm something of a quantum anomaly. The ordinary laws of physics don't fully apply to me. You've inherited some of my warped physics. It's taken a long time for your abilities to manifest, but you apparently have the ability to generate microscopic wormholes. Since the strongest gravity well in the neighborhood is the sun, the other ends of the wormholes tend to congregate there. Thus, when you open these wormholes, you're unleashing pure solar material here on earth. Keep in mind, these wormholes are very tiny. If you only opened one or two, we'd probably need sensitive instruments to detect the effect. Open a few thousand over a diffuse area and you get scorched sheets. Open a few million in the palm of your hand, and poof, dead nun."

Sunday rose up from the hot sand, brushing her bare knees clean.

"If you're my real father, why has my mother never mentioned you?"

Monday shrugged. "I raped her. That scar on her right eyebrow? I gave her that. She probably doesn't like to talk about it."

Sunday felt her guts tighten. "What kind of monster are you?"

"Oh, the very worst kind," said Monday. "There are two types of monsters. There are things that are less than human. And there are things that are more than human. I'm in the second category. Everyone is alive because of me. Since I created life, I feel no remorse about ending it. What I want, I take, since, really, everything is mine. I wanted your mother, so I took her. Now I want you."

Sunday gave him the fiercest look she could summon. "Touch me and I'll burn you."

"No," said Monday, with a dismissive wave. "I don't mean I want you like that. I want you as a soldier. I want to make use of your power in my ongoing war."

"You kill three cops, kidnap me, and brag about raping my mother," Sunday said, surprising herself with how calmly she recited this list. "Why, exactly, would I help you?"

Monday shrugged. "Do you have a better use for your time? You're a nun-killer. Fair or not, you'll get some of the blame for those three dead cops. For the rest of your life, you're going to be hunted. You can't go back to your mother. You can't go out and get a normal job. You're never going to have a house of your own, or a boyfriend, or any friends at all, once they find out the truth about you. Your life in the ordinary world is over."

"So what?" asked Sunday. "Am I supposed to just kill myself?"

"No. You're supposed to come live in the extraordinary world. You aren't my only child. All of you have powers. I've already harnessed the power of two of my children, a boy who causes panic and a particularly nasty little freak I call Baby Gun. Since you set things on fire, I was thinking it would be appropriate to call you Baby Burn."

"I'm nobody's baby," said Sunday, clenching her fists.

"Suit yourself. The name's not important. All that's important is your power. With one possible exception, I believe you've the potential to be the strongest of all my offspring. Given full command of your powers, you could reduce this desert to glass for a hundred miles in every direction. You could destroy cities with but a thought. I am not a kind and loving God. You will be the instrument of my wrath."

"Maybe I don't want to burn cities," said Sunday. "I didn't mean to kill that nun."

"You're still young," said Monday. "Let me show you the world. By the end of the tour, you'll hate all mankind."

Sunday locked her jaw to keep from speaking. She didn't want to confess she was halfway there. She'd had a string of stepfathers, each more stupid and mean than their predecessor. She hated them all, and she hated her mother even more for being too weak and foolish not to see the destruction she was bringing on herself by falling for these losers. As Sunday had grown older, her mother's stupidity seemed very much to be the pattern of the world. She could see it in all her schoolmates, each with their own unique mix of stupidity, cruelty, weakness and vanity.

Despite her general contempt for mankind, Sunday wasn't a murderer. At least, not on purpose. But should she tell Monday that? She decided she would try another tactic to get him to leave her alone. She crossed her arms. "I'm afraid you're wasting your time. I can't melt cities. I can't even melt a fucking camera so I can use the bathroom in private."

"You probably are a waste of my time," said Monday. "Almost everything is. But we both know you can melt a camera. You just wouldn't."

"I tried."

"Trying is the wrong technique. You first began to manifest your powers during the throes of sexual release, when your mind was wiped blank by pleasure."

Sunday wrinkled her nose. "How can you know that?"

"Please," said Monday. "If I can build a machine to take me anyplace in the world, don't you think I can build one to let me watch anyone in the world? If you'd gone to the bathroom in the jail, it would have simply joined the thousands of hours of similar recordings I've made of you."

"You bastard!" she said, pushing her hands toward him. She hoped a wall of flame would sweep out and vaporize him. It didn't.

Monday sighed. "Very dramatic. But also very cerebral. You've done very well in your studies over the years, despite a long history of behavioral problems. You've scored as high as 156 on IQ scores. You're good at thinking. I need you to be good at emotion. I need anger! I need hate!"

"I'm as pissed off as I've ever been right now!" she growled, shaking her fist. But was she? She'd always been introspective, even detached. She often felt like an actress playing the role of Sunday. She was constantly improvising her lines. But did she really feel them?

She once more pointed her arms at Monday. "Burn!" she screamed, and tried to blast the man with the full force of her anger.

Monday stared at her silently, waiting for flames that never came. A moment later, he shook his head. "Pathetic." He pulled the calculator out of his shirt pocket. "If you can't use your powers, you're of no use to me. Unfortunately, I've revealed too much about myself to let you live."

"For what it's worth, I haven't understood even half of what you've said."

"No one ever does," said Monday, punching in a series of numbers.

Suddenly, there was an old man standing to his right. He looked like a bum, in worn and dirty clothes, his thin hair unwashed, his face covered in gray stubble. He stank so badly Sunday's eyes watered from ten feet away.

The bum dropped to his knees and let out a loud retching sound, though nothing but a long line of yellowish spit came from his mouth.

"Christ almighty," the bum whimpered, wiping his lips. "No disrespect, Mr. Monday, but can't you give me a warning 'fore you do that?"

"Stop whining and get on your feet. I need you to eat my daughter."

The bum rose on wobbly legs, eying Sunday with confusion.

"Your daughter?"

"Eat her," said Monday.

"Excuse me?" said Sunday. "Is this some kind of weird not-quite-rape threat?"

"No," said Monday. "I found my associate here working at a carnival in Mexico. He's a geek. If you're unfamiliar with that particular act, it means that he was the wild man in a pit who bit the heads off chickens. Only, this freak could suck down an entire goat in one bite. They called him El Chupacabra. Since he doesn't remember his real name, I've taken to calling him Pit Geek."

"Just so I'm straight on this, you think he's going to eat me like he ate a goat?" Sunday really wasn't sure if this was supposed to be menacing, or just the least funny joke she'd ever heard.

"I've watched Pit Geek swallow an entire crane before. He

can handle you."

"Crane? Like the bird?"

"Like the thing they use to build skyscrapers."

Sunday's confusion evidently showed in her face, because Monday added, "For some reason, he generates space warps as he chews, and can suck down anything. I'm still puzzling out the exact source of his powers."

"He looks too old to be your kid," said Sunday.

"Indeed. He's a mystery. One day I'll solve that mystery for him, as long as he obeys me."

Pit Geek sighed loudly and scratched his head. "Well, sir, you're right that I don't know much about myself. And I'd really like to find out who I am, or who I used to be. But one thing I do know, Mr. Monday, is that I ain't gonna swallow no little girl."

"She's no longer a little girl," said Monday. "She's been menstruating for almost four years. She's biologically as much of an adult as you are. Eat her."

"Can we leave my biology out of this?" asked Sunday.

Pit Geek shrugged. "Kid, you might think about running."

"Fucking useless goatsucker," Monday mumbled as he punched in more coordinates. He pointed toward Sunday in with a rather melodramatic pose and shouted, "Crush her!"

Sunday looked up. There was now a two hundred foot tall baby doll standing next to Rex Monday. The flesh was a little too pink to be life-like. The doll had a flabby toddler body, and jutting from his shoulders where his head should have been there was an old fashioned revolver the size of a school bus. Perhaps the masculine symbolism of the gun explained why she thought of the giant as male. In truth, the monster's crotch was as smooth and featureless as the dunes that surrounded them.

"You must be Baby Gun," she said.

There was a flash of light.

A loud boom followed instantaneously, followed by the *tink tink tink* tink of a thousand bits of shrapnel landing on the black glass around her. It was suddenly daylight in the desert. Sunday had her hands raised over her head. She'd just blown a bullet the size of a sports car to smithereens before it touched her. She'd vaporized her clothes as a result. But since both Pit Geek and Rex Monday had their hands over their eyes, she was apparently glowing too brightly for them to see anything. Which was a relief, since in addition to being naked, she'd also lost control of her bladder.

Above her, the giant revolver clicked to the next chamber. She ran, still glowing, but uncertain she could blow apart a second bullet when she really hadn't even seen the first one. She was thrown from her feet as the bullet slammed into the ground behind her. She crashed into the sand seconds later. It splashed like liquid as her heat melted the ground into a goopy bubbling syrup.

She struggled to rise in the molten slop as the hair rose on the back of her neck. She looked up to see Baby Gun's enormous foot falling toward her. She lifted her hand and touched his heel as it fell. It felt like it was made of rubber. Then it wasn't made of anything, as the solar flare that spilled out of her fingers tore the leg into a slurry of elemental particles. The giant toppled, crashing into the dunes. The air stank of burning plastic.

Sunday sat up, studying the flickering plasma that sheathed her. She giggled. "Not half bad! Bring me another nun!"

Rex Monday stomped toward her, pressing a button on his belt. By the time he reached her, his clothes and skin were coated in a thin sheen of what looked like Vaseline, though Sunday was pretty sure Vaseline would have burned.

Monday grabbed her by the wrist and yanked her back to her feet.

"Sorry I broke your doll," she said, in the most taunting tone she could summon.

"You ran from the bullet!" Monday screamed, then slapped her.

Sunday placed a hand on her cheek as the flames around her grew brighter. None of her stepfathers had ever struck her. The pain was such a surprise she didn't know how to react.

"You should be able to fly!" Monday snarled, striking her

again, this time with his knuckles cutting into her eyebrow. She raised her arms to block further blows and he kicked her in the gut. "You think half good is good enough? You should be able to shoot into the air like a rocket! You still aren't in control!"

"Make up your damned mind!" Sunday screamed. "You told me I needed to lose cont—" Her protest was cut short when he slammed his fist into her lips. She fell back on the sand, blinking away tears. He drove his foot down on her left breast with such force if felt as if he'd bruised her heart.

She could barely breathe as he leaned down and grabbed her by the hair. He pulled her into a seating position and raised his hand to strike her face once more. Sunday closed her eyes.

The blow never came.

She opened her eyes and found that Pit Geek was holding Monday's arm.

"Mr. Monday, calm down. She's your flesh and blood. Don't kill her!"

Monday responded by pulling the pistol out of his back pocket and shooting Pit Geek in the center of his chest. The old bum dropped back onto the sand, limp.

"You killed him!" Sunday said, though why she felt shocked by this she couldn't quite say.

"I wish," grumbled Monday, as Pit Geek flopped his arms around uselessly. "As near as I can tell, he's immortal. He's shrugged off worse than a bullet."

Monday glared down at Sunday. Then he smiled. "With your face bleeding like that, you remind me of your mother."

Sunday growled. Monday disappeared in a maelstrom of swirling light. The radiance was so great that even she couldn't see what was happening. Three seconds later, when the flash of fury faded away and her eyes adjusted, she discovered she was roughly three hundred feet in the air. Pit Geek and Rex Monday looked like little bugs. To her disappointment, Monday was unscathed by the maelstrom she'd unleashed, though Pit Geek was now rolling around in the scalding sand, his clothes on fire.

Rex Monday looked up at her. Once more, he beamed with

pride. He gave her a thumb's up.

"Welcome to the family," he shouted.

She blinked away the blood that trickled into her eyes. Flying felt . . . well, it felt like lying on a really, really wobbly under-inflated air mattress. She was spread-eagled, like a paratrooper in freefall, only she wasn't falling. The slightest motion of her hands or feet sent her skittering across the sky. She felt insanely unsteady and unsafe, both in body and soul.

She hated Rex Monday. She hated that she'd failed to kill him with her fire. But a part of her felt a strange, pathetic gratitude toward the creep. Not even in her wildest imagination had she thought that scorch marks on her sheets were evidence that she could fly.

She could fly.

There were two kinds of monsters. Those who were less than human. And those who were more.

Doing her best to maintain her balance, she looked around the heavens until she found the Big Dipper, and used this to find the North Star. If this really was the Sahara, she need only fly in that direction to make it to Europe. She might even wind up in Spain, and she spoke Spanish, at least a little. Maybe Rex Monday wouldn't find her there. Maybe she could still have an ordinary life.

Or maybe she should try to land and talk more to the man who'd known she could fly. She gazed at the ground. The giant doll's leg looked like it was growing back. Pit Geek was back on his feet, looking barely inconvenienced by a hole in his chest and third degree burns to his legs.

Going back down to a known murderer who'd just beaten her was the dumbest thing she could possibly do, and Sunday was anything but dumb. But Sunday couldn't shake the feeling this had all been a carefully staged lesson, designed to trigger her powers and teach her how to use them. Rex Monday had just blasted away whole mountains of her ignorance regarding her abilities. What more might Rex Monday teach her?

Bringing her arms closer to her sides, she reduced the thrust that held her in the air and descended toward the man who claimed to be her father. Whether it was true or not didn't matter. He was a violent psychopath with delusions of grandeur. She'd never trust him. But how could she turn her back on the man who'd just given her the sky?

Found a typewriter in the rubble today.
Beaten up, but it works. Remington. Seems
old. The keys are perfectly round,
yellowed with age. The ribbon barely
leaves a mark on the brown sheets of
grocery bag paper.
There's something sentimental about the
keys clicking. I remember sitting in a
hot room. It's an attic somewhere; the
walls are made of beadboard, painted pale
puke green. There's an oil lamp hanging
on the hook next to me, unlit. The
daylight is slowly fading out the window.
A dingy white curtain hangs limp in the
stale air. For as far as the eye can see,
there's wasteland, little scrub bushes,
dust and rocks everywhere, flat as can
be. There's a bottle of tequila on the
desk next to the typewriter, a bowl of
limes, a knife.
I'd taken my bike out to the high desert
to find words. I'd gone to write a new
story.
I'd gone to become a new man.
I'd still believed then, still believed
in the redeeming power of stories.
But story's just another word for lie.

Chapter Two
The Beast of Bladenboro

Today

BLADENBORO, NORTH CAROLINA, can fairly be described as the middle of nowhere. Its sits on a crossroads of two highways that few people travel. To the west lies Butters, south is Boardman, east is Clarkton and north is Dublin, but not the Dublin you've heard of. The primary thing you'd remember about Bladenboro was how flat it was, surrounded by yellow dirt fields planted with soybeans, amid countless miles of pine forest. Beyond the trees, meandering creeks wound through long patches of swampland.

Bladenboro's only claim to fame was its monster. Starting back in the 1950s, residents reported livestock disappearing. What bodies were discovered were mangled with strange wounds, the eyes and genitals removed with nearly surgical precision. By the sixties the reports fell off, and by the turn of the century hardly anybody remembered the Beast of Bladenboro.

But two years ago goats started disappearing again. Or at least, parts of them. Farmers would find the back half of a goat lying in their pen, the front half nowhere to be seen. Bones weren't crushed or even scratched by whatever chopped the goats in two. The severing was as clean and neat as if an industrial laser had carved up the beast.

The History Channel came to town and shot some footage of the surrounding swamps for their new *Alien Hunter* series. They had the bad luck to arrive on a week that no animals were reported killed. They left with some old photos and lots of footage of shadowy forests and edited together a one-hour special on the beast. After it aired, amateur monster hunters would arrive in town and traipse around the swamps with night vision goggles, taping motion-sensitive cameras to every other tree. They got a lot of pictures of deer and more than a few snapshots of startled hunters.

Bucky Cheraw was one of those hunters and he was glad when deer season came around again. By now, the nut jobs had moved on to a fresh alien sighting in West Virginia. The woods around Bladenboro were quiet once more. The only people out here were other hunters smart enough to wear orange vests, not those yahoos from the city who'd been stupid enough to run around the woods in tan and brown, almost begging to get shot.

It was a cool September morning just before dawn when Bucky parked his truck at the end of the logging road and began traipsing into the pines armed with a hunting bow. Bow season started a few weeks before the regular season, and he liked getting a shot at the really big bucks before the less ambitious hunters started stomping through the forest and spooking all the deer.

Bucky's deer stand was only about a mile from where he'd parked. He'd built it himself, treehouse style in a big maple, not wasting a dime on those fancy aluminum stands some hunters used. He considered himself a traditionalist, inheritor of a hunting heritage that dated back a thousand years among the Lumbee Indians with whom his ancestors had intermarried. Of course, his ancestors might not have recognized his airplane-grade aluminum arrow shafts with the titanium hunting heads, nor the laser scope he used to target his shots. Bucky was the first to argue that being traditionalist didn't mean you had to be a primitive.

A hundred yards from his hunting stand, Bucky caught whiff of rotting meat. He looked up into the dark branches above him and spotted black shapes like gargoyles silhouetted against the brightening sky. Buzzards. Pausing so that he no longer heard the sound of his feet crunching through the leaves, he could hear buzzards flapping around on the ground in the distance. He headed their way out of idle curiosity.

He found the large gray birds picking apart a brown lump on the ground. They hopped and fluttered across the dry pine needles as he approached, backing off but not abandoning their prize completely. Bucky pressed his mouth and nose into the sleeve of his coat in an attempt to cut down the stench.

The thing had obviously been a deer, probably a buck, though by now the buzzards had picked apart the genitals so thoroughly he couldn't be sure. Complicating identification further, the front half of the deer was simply gone.

Where was a crew from the History Channel when you needed one?

He left the area slightly spooked, but only slightly. It made more sense to believe in poachers than to believe in aliens. A man had probably killed the deer ahead of season. He kept the head for a trophy and had probably started butchering the animal, cutting off its front half with a chainsaw. This wasn't the technique Bucky would have used to butcher a deer, but hey, they were poachers. If they'd been bright, they would have carried out the hindquarters first, since that's where the good meat was. Instead, they'd probably carted out the front quarters, then spotted a game warden and gotten spooked. Case closed. Mystery solved.

The only monsters skulking around these woods were lawless men.

Fortunately, his hunting blind was upwind of the stink. He studied the old pin oak that held the blind, wondering if he should trim a few of the low hanging branches to improve his view of the target area. The tree was situated where the woods thinned out at the border of a field. Running along the edge of this field was an irrigation ditch. Deer would congregate to chew the greenery around the ditch and get a drink. It was a rare day he didn't spot at least a dozen deer. The true skill lay in simply having the patience to wait for the right trophy buck to come along.

Bucky reached the wooden ladder that led up into his blind. He stopped and stared up.

Someone was snoring.

Someone was asleep in the blind.

The blind was just barely big enough for a grown man to lie down in if he stretched from one corner to the other of the five by five square platform. The blind was about fifteen feet off the ground, with the back wall away from the field completely open and a couple of long narrow windows on the other walls for him to line up his shots. He stepped back, standing on his tiptoes to see who was inside, but couldn't get the right angle to see beyond the edge of the floor.

Maybe it wasn't a man. Did raccoons snore? Did skunks? What else could go up a tree like that?

If it was a skunk, he didn't want to startle it. On the other hand, he didn't want to waste a lot of time. The sun was up proper now and the golden hour for hunting was underway.

But what if it was a man? Could it be someone he knew? Some local teen maybe, who'd found the tree house a convenient hiding place for getting drunk? Or maybe some other hunter who'd wandered this way to find him, got here early, gone up and fallen asleep waiting?

Or a convict. While he hadn't heard any news, what if someone had escaped from the prison over in Lumberton? What better place to hide than here in these woods? If it was a prisoner, he'd be desperate. Dangerous. Should he call the sheriff?

On the other hand, he'd be a laughing stock if he called the sheriff and it turned out to be a noisy raccoon.

Bucky wondered what his proud Lumbee ancestors would have done. So, he hid behind a tree and let out a loud "Whoop! Whoop! Whoop!"

The snoring stopped.

The boards of the blind creaked as something heavy began to stir.

Then, a man's voice: "Christ almighty."

Bucky placed an arrow against his bowstring. If the man had a gun, he'd have to let loose a shot in the space of a heartbeat. He stepped from behind the tree.

A gray haired man was sitting in the blind, his bare feet dangling over the edge. The legs of his pants were little more than tatters. He was wearing a green flannel shirt matted with dark blood. His face was nightmarish; it looked as if someone had attacked the man with an axe and split his face in two, and the two halves hadn't been lined up properly before they were stitched back together. A line of thick scabs ran down the middle of the man's face, oozing puss. The man's bleary eyes were unfocused; he hadn't spotted Bucky, though Bucky was standing in plain sight wearing a bright orange jacket.

"Who are you?" Bucky called out, drawing the arrow back to a firing position, but not yet aiming it toward the man.

The stranger scratched his thin gray hair as he looked in Bucky's direction. One eye seemed to sit a half-inch lower than the other, but finally both eyes spotted him. "Well now, I don't rightly know."

"What do you mean you don't know?"

"I've had kind of a rough time of late," said the man. "Got my head split open. Lot of memories spilled out."

"If you were in a fight, the sheriff probably has a report of it," said Bucky. "Come down and I'll call him. He can help you out."

"Naw," said the stranger, shaking his head. "Don't need the law involved."

"You a fugitive?" asked Bucky.

"What kind of question is that?" asked the man. "If I was, why would I tell you? And if I ain't, why would you believe me if I say I ain't? It's like me asking if you're still beating your wife."

"I'm not married," said Bucky.

"Well I ain't either," said the stranger. "You and me, we could be buddies. Pal around. You know a place 'round here we could go drink beer and watch women take their clothes off?"

"I think you've had enough beer," said Bucky. He slowly released the tension on his arrow. The stranger didn't look like he was armed, and was too groggy to climb down from the tree. Convict or not, this land belonged to Bucky's second

25

cousin and the stranger was trespassing. He pulled his cell phone from his vest pocket.

"Aw, don't call the cops," said the stranger. "Can't you be cool?"

"I'm practically cold," said Bucky. "I'm doing you a favor. You need medical attention."

"What? 'Cause of my face? Shoot. It would heal if I'd stop picking at it."

Bucky dialed the phone.

The stranger rose, perched precariously on the edge of the platform. "I asked you nicely not to call the law."

"You just sit down before you fall and hurt yourself," said Bucky as the phone began to ring on the other end.

The man stepped forward, seeming to forget where he was and crashed into the ground fifteen feet below with a loud *THUMP*.

"Shit!" said Bucky.

"Excuse me?" said Sally Henderson on the other end of the phone. He'd known Sally since high school. She was one of the dispatchers for the Sheriff's Department.

"Sally, it's Bucky Cheraw!"

"Bucky! How are you this fine morning!"

"It's weird one, Sally. I'm out at Billy's farm where I do my hunting. When I got here, I found some homeless guy asleep in my stand. He might be a fugitive; he didn't want me to call you."

"Where's he at now?"

"Not fifty feet in front of me and he might be dead. He fell out of my blind right before I called and he didn't look none to healthy to start with."

"I'll get an ambulance out there immediately. I'll send out Deputy Tucker as well."

"Thank you, Sally."

"No problem. Want me to stay on the line until they get there?"

"Ah, I guess not," said Bucky. He didn't want to sound like he needed somebody to hold his hand though this. "You got other calls to take."

"Probably," said Sally. "First day of bow season. Always at least one call of somebody getting hurt. You take care."

"Take care now," said Bucky, hanging up.

The second he put the phone back into his pocket, the stranger stirred. A fifteen-foot fall onto concrete might kill a man, but on soft ground Bucky wasn't surprised the man was all right. He drew his bow and took aim as the man sat up.

"Don't move a muscle," said Bucky. "The law and an ambulance are on their way."

The man shook his head and sighed. "Mister, I don't remember killing anybody for almost three months now. You're about to make me ruin a perfectly good streak."

"The only thing I'm going to do is put an arrow through your neck if you try to stand up."

The man stood up.

Bucky's laser sight had a perfect red dot an inch to the left of the man's Adam's apple. He let go of the arrow, certain it would hit the carotid artery. On a deer, this would be the ultimate kill shot, dropping a buck where it stood.

The arrow found its mark, coming to rest with the tip of the arrow jutting out a good foot from the back of the man's neck. Dark blood trickled down his throat in a ketchup-slow ooze. The stranger sighed, but didn't fall down. He reached behind his neck and drew the arrow all the way through, then tossed it to the ground.

"I bet about now, the beer and nekkid dancers look like the smarter choice," the man said, his voice little more than a faint gurgle.

Bucky drew another arrow. The man walked toward him. The arrow came to a stop deep in the man's left breast. The man stumbled, but kept on his feet, still moving forward.

"Christ almighty," he said. "I wish you knew how bad that stings."

Bucky dropped his bow and spun on his heels. He leaned forward to run but not before the stranger grabbed him by the collar. He spun around in the man's grasp, reaching for the hunting knife in his belt. He snapped the sheath open, but in his panic nearly dropped the knife. With a shaking hand he thrust upward, driving the blade into the man's gut.

The man grinned at him. His breath was rancid as he asked, "How's that stabbing working out for ya?"

Bucky reared back to punch the man in the face. His fist flew toward the man's ragged, rotting teeth. An instant before his hand hit, the man opened his mouth. It seemed no bigger than an ordinary mouth, but somehow Bucky's fist seemed to shrink as it slipped between the teeth, vanishing all the way down to the bicep. He paused, feeling as is his fist should now be a good foot and a half out the back of the stranger's head.

He wiggled his fingers. He didn't feel guts or tongue. He didn't feel anything but empty air.

The stranger had a twinkle in his eye as he said, "Nuh uh guh tuh tuh scruh!"

Then he bit down, and Bucky's arm disappeared just above the elbow. Bucky stumbled backward, blood gushing from his severed arteries. He slipped and fell on the leafy forest floor. He clamped his good hand over his stump, squeezing to slow the bleeding.

The stranger chuckled as he plucked the arrow from his chest. "I said, 'Now's a good time to scream!'"

Bucky didn't scream. He whimpered. "What the hell are you?"

"I wish to God I knew," said the man. The stranger leaned down and grabbed Bucky's left boot. "I could use some new shoes."

Bucky kicked the man's hands away with his free leg.

The stranger sighed. "Look, you shot me in the neck and chest, and knifed me in the guts. All I did was bite you one time. Hell, you got a good shot of living if you don't fight me. Fifty-fifty, maybe. That ambulance is going to show up and whisk you off to whatever hospital is near here. Is there a hospital near here?"

"Lumberton," Bucky said through clenched teeth.

"Sure, that's right," said the man, scratching his head. "Damn, I wish I could think straight. We're in North Carolina?"

"Yeah," said Bucky, feeling dizzy.

"Almost there, then." The stranger looked around. "You got a truck or something nearby?"

"That way," Bucky pointed with a nod of his head. "About a mile."

"I'm guessing the keys are in your pants?"

Bucky nodded.

"Hold still. I'm taking your pants. Play nice and I'll give you your arm back."

"What are you . . . ?"

"Just hold still," the man said, squatting down, untying Bucky's boot. Bucky felt too lightheaded to resist. At this point, all he wanted was for the man to go away. He said nothing as the stranger stripped him of his boots and socks and pants. Time slowed to a crawl as he listened, desperately hoping for the wail of sirens.

Dark spots danced before his eyes as the stranger finished getting dressed.

Perhaps his eyes played tricks on him, but as the man tightened his stolen belt, he looked down at Bucky with a look approaching pity. He reached his hand into his mouth, his arm vanishing up to the elbow. A second later, he pulled out Bucky's arm. He dropped it into the dirt next to Bucky.

"Next time," the man said, "don't shoot first and ask questions later."

"I asked lots of questions first," Bucky mumbled.

The man rubbed his stubbled chin. "You know, I reckon you did. Never mind, then."

He turned and walked through the woods, his boots crunching loudly. Bucky inched his way toward a tree and managed to sit up. No matter how tightly he squeezed his arm, there was blood seeping out with each heartbeat. He looked toward the field. Help would probably come from that direction, coming up the field road instead of coming in from the back along the logging road. He rolled forward, he face landing next to his severed arm. He reached out and grabbed the sleeve of his camo jacket in his teeth. With superhuman will, he managed to rise and take a dozen stumbling steps toward the field, where he tumbled into the ditch. He rolled to a stop, face up, staring at the morning sky. There was a loud ringing in his ears, but no sirens.

Along the tree line, against the pale blue heavens, vultures gathered.

Nothing rots here. I'm not sure time
passes at the same rate. I look out at
the ring, like a miniature Saturn without
a planet at the center, made of junk and
carrion, and wonder if we're in motion.
There are no stars against which to
measure our movement. The sky is pale
white in all directions except the core,
which is too bright to look at.
I've found three different clocks. All
were electric. It's a shame I never got
my hands on an hourglass. But then, what
could I prove? Perhaps the passing of an
hour here measures eons elsewhere.
I had plenty of chances to swallow the
one man who might have been able to think
this through. But I probably would have
spit him back out. Monday always seemed
kind of bitter.

Chapter Three
A Leg to Stand On

SUNDAY PULLED her rented Toyota Camry into the parking lot of the post office in Georgetown, South Carolina. It was November 11, and this was the next to last town on the contact list. Long before they'd been blamed for destroying Jerusalem, Rex Monday had explained that there might come a time when they would have to lie low. He'd told Sunday not to think of hiding and waiting as a form of retreat. In asymmetrical warfare, not attacking was a legitimate strategy. While you conserved your strength, the enemy spent more and more resources to less and less effect. The resources required to scan ten million suitcases for bombs cost exactly the same if there were no bombs as if there were a thousand. In fact, no bombs can be an even greater weapon than a thousand bombs. If one bomb a month were discovered at an airport, the level of vigilance would remain high. No one would question the value of the resources spent. But if no bombs turn up year after year, complacency would set in. The public would view security as a burden imposed upon them rather than a right they are entitled to. Political rifts would form over the wisdom of spending money to protect citizens from a seemingly imaginary foe.

Sunday was early. They weren't supposed to meet at the post office box until 11:11am. Pit Geek still had ten minutes to arrive, assuming he was still alive. He hadn't made it to the checkpoint last year in Vegas.

Georgetown was about as different from Vegas as you could get. It was a small town that prided itself on a lot of old buildings. Sunday wasn't impressed by three-hundred-year-old brick houses, graveyards filled with worn tombstones, or streets lined with towering oaks draped with Spanish moss. Even Vegas, where everything was new, had fallen for the weak-minded nostalgia of trying to make things look old. It was further proof that human evolution had reached a dead end. Once the species became so weak-minded it focused all its energy on the past, it had nothing left to carry it into the future.

Sunday was in this pathetic little town only because Monday had arranged their check-ins in places with significant tourist populations. Georgetown was a small port on the South Carolina coast at about the midpoint between Myrtle Beach and Charleston. A steady stream of visitors stopped downtown to browse through antique stores and partake of the local eateries on the waterfront. Though she was a stranger in town, no one would give her a second glance.

She got out of the car at 11:10. Pit Geek was almost certainly dead, assuming he could die. She would miss him. Though she'd found him physically repulsive, she'd enjoyed his dry sense of humor and his curiously convoluted moral code. He was a cold-blooded killer who would murder a man for looking at him funny. She knew that he'd once helped plant bombs on school buses, so he had no moral qualms about killing children. It was difficult to reconcile this with the man who'd grabbed Rex Monday's arm to stop him from beating her. She'd asked about it once. He'd shrugged like the question didn't make sense. "A job's a job and a war's a war," he'd said. "But I never had no stomach for bullies."

She went into the post office and fit the key into box 111. Inside was a pink slip informing her she had a package at the window. The line was ten people deep. She sighed and took her place in the queue. For not the first time, she thought about disobeying her father's orders. She could just kill everyone in the building and grab the package, then fly off and be in the Bahamas by nightfall. But, no, she was lying low. She was engaging in warfare by other means.

A little girl about four years old was in line in front of her, along with her mother, a heavy set black woman in her twenties. The little girl stared at Sunday's ankles. Then she announced, "She's got a robot leg."

Sunday felt everyone's eyes turn toward her. She was wearing pants, but no socks, and her c-leg was showing where it fit into her deck shoes. Just above the shoe, little more showed than a slender silver rod. She'd lost her leg at the battle of Jerusalem and had been wearing the prosthetic so long she sometimes forgot about it.

"Don't be rude," said the mother to the little girl. She gave Sunday an apologetic glance. "Kids," she said, as if this were enough explanation.

Behind the counter, Sunday noticed one of the postal workers disappear into an office.

One dangerous flaw in Rex Monday's advance planning was that checking their annual instructions required Sunday and Pit Geek to go into buildings where their pictures hung on the wall. They were on both the FBI's most wanted plus the Department of Planetary Security's list of suspected hostile aliens. She found her presence on that list amusing. Her father had introduced her to a few of the dozen or so actual aliens who lived on earth, and none of them had made the list, despite actually looking like aliens. Jon Zeno in Brooklyn had fangs, scales, three eyes, and a horn growing out of his forehead. He breathed from a tank filled with ammonia and he'd still been cleared by the agency as a body modification artist.

Luckily Sunday had the sort of face that people didn't dwell on. So many Hispanic immigrants had flooded into the southern US in the last twenty years that her dark skin didn't merit a second glance. Her eyebrows were a bit thicker than most women's, but aside from this her face was rather unremarkable, neither ugly nor pretty, just plain. In the one good picture the FBI had of her, she'd been sporting a nose-ring and gone heavy on the mascara that day. She'd stopped wearing jewelry years ago and didn't even own make up any more. She'd discovered that this rendered her almost invisible.

And then there was her leg. Thanks to the various wars Monday had help set in motion, the number of veterans sporting artificial limbs was swelling by thousands each year.

Still, there were far more men than women with artificial limbs. The leg was enough to make people give her a second glance.

She kept watching the office as the line crept forward. She glanced around at the surveillance cameras. She stared at the package slip. After so many years with no word from her father, was it suspicious that this slip turned up now? Was this a set up? If they'd captured Pit Geek, would he have told them the rendezvous points?

She made it to the counter. She traded her slip for a box roughly the size of a toaster oven.

She left the post office with as casual a pace as she could muster. What the hell was in the box? Were her years of hiding finally at an end?

There was now a pickup truck parked beside her Camry. The sunlight on the windshield hid the driver's face, but she could tell from his silhouette that he was watching her. The door swung open, and the ugliest man she'd ever seen stepped out. At a second glance, she recognized him.

"Pete!" she exclaimed, running toward him.

He furrowed his brow. "Am I Pete?"

She drew within an arm's length and said, quietly, "You are in public. People look at you funny if I call you 'Pit.' Not that people aren't going to look at you funny with your face messed up like this. Get in the car before people start talking."

Pit started to get back into his truck. She grabbed his arm. "No, you idiot. My car. I've checked it for tracers. You didn't do that on your truck, did you?"

"How the hell would I know what a tracer looked like?" Pit asked as she dragged him to the Camry. She opened the passenger door and shoved him in, then threw the package into the back seat. As it left her fingers, she wondered if it might be some sort of doomsday device deserving of more delicate treatment. When the world failed to end by the time she closed the door, she relaxed. Two minutes later, they were at the Georgetown city limits, not because was going fast, but because Georgetown just wasn't that big.

"Where the hell have you been?" she asked. "What happened

to your face?"

"Lots of places," Pit said. "Don't remember 'em all. I kind of remember holding the right half of my head in my hands then jamming it back on. Might've jumped into some helicopter blades? Look before you leap. Good advice."

"How did you remember to come here today?"

Pit shrugged. "Dunno. My brain is still kind of splicing itself back together. Sometimes I know stuff without knowing why I know it. I knew I had to be at the Georgetown post office on November 11 at 11:11. Couldn't remember if it was a.m. or p.m. Took a guess."

"Do you remember my father? Rex Monday?"

Pit frowned. "He was that terrorist guy in the news a few years back. He was your father? Whatever happened to him?"

"We don't know what happened to him! That's the point of us meeting at different post offices every year. We're waiting for further instructions."

"Oh," said Pit. He gave her a long stare. "I know I know you. I remember . . . you carried me around in . . . I dunno . . . a basket? Like a baby? Are you . . . are you my mother?"

She gave him a sideways glance. "You're joking, right?"

"I look older than you, so it doesn't make sense. But . . . I was little."

"You were decapitated at the battle of Jerusalem. A hand grenade blew your body into hamburger but your head bounced free. You were still alive. It took you months to regrow your body. For a long time, I was carrying your head around in a cooler. Later, when you had a little toddler body and a full sized head, we used a baby carriage. But once you could walk, we went our separate ways. We were a much more vulnerable target together than apart."

Pit nodded. "I was shot in the neck and chest a little over a month ago. Hurt like hell, but now I just have little scars left. Do you know why I can heal from stuff like this?"

"No. And for what it's worth, you didn't know why you couldn't die when I first met you, almost ten years ago. Your memory's been crap the whole time I've known you. You seem to have a talent for head injuries. But as far as I know, you're immortal."

"Naw," he said. "Can't be."

"Why not?"

He sighed. "I may not pay taxes, but I ain't kidding myself about death. I don't know much, but I do know the world's a bitch. No one gets out alive."

Sunday chuckled. "Hell, Pit, for a brain-damaged freak, that almost makes sense."

Pit looked out the window. "Maybe I was born this way. Brain-damaged, I mean. Maybe I've always been stupid."

"Maybe," said Sunday. It wasn't her responsibility to cheer Pit up.

"So," he said. "You got a name?"

"My code name was Sundancer. You used to call me Sunny. But my given name is Sunday."

Pit looked skeptical.

"What?" she asked.

"Your name is Sunday Monday?"

She sighed. They had a long drive ahead of them.

BY THE TIME they'd reached Virginia, she felt less paranoid. She assumed that no one at the Post Office had deduced that the twenty-five year old Hispanic woman with the c-leg was the same twenty-five year old Hispanic woman with a c-leg currently hunted for a long list of crimes against humanity. In a way, she felt contempt that she hadn't been found out. It wasn't difficult to hide in plain sight. Most Americans were too busy staring at their cell phones to pay any attention to the wanted criminals who moved among them.

They checked into a motel room in Petersburg, Virginia. It was a no-name, mom and pop place. The old man at the desk didn't bat an eye when she'd paid in cash. In what was likely pure coincidence, they were given room 11.

Pit closed the door behind them as Sunday placed the package on the bed. She carefully removed the tape and opened the cardboard, revealing a block of Styrofoam. She slid this out of the box and pulled the two halves apart.

Inside was a gun about eighteen inches long that looked as if it had been designed for a Star Wars movie. It was made of almost as much glass as metal. The side of the barrel was covered in vents. Where the trigger should be, there was a round, flat button.

"I bet it's some kind of death ray," said Pit. "Wasn't the boss always talking about a death ray?"

"Nope. He used to say that he didn't need a death ray because he had me," said Sunday.

Pit's eyes lit up. "Yeah. You . . . you shoot out fire from your hands. And you can fly. I remember now."

There was a note in the box.

My teleportation belt wasn't a complete waste after all. Presenting the Regeneration Ray! May you always have a leg to stand on.

Then, a postscript: *P.S. War is over.*

"War is over?" she muttered.

"What war?" asked Pit.

She read him the note.

"What war?" he asked again.

"How can you not remember?" she asked. "We were branded terrorists because we were trying to topple the governments of the world."

"Which ones?"

"All of them," said Sunday. "The entire world was corrupted by the machinations of my father's enemies. There was no hope of repairing it piecemeal. We had to cripple every last remnant of the old order so that my father could finally become the true rex mundi."

Pit looked puzzled.

"Rex mundi is Latin for king of the world."

Pit nodded. "Yeah. Sure. Didn't . . . did we tear down the Washington Monument?"

"Almost."

"And . . . and the Twin Towers?"

"Not us, actually."

"Jerusalem? We destroyed it?"

"Helped, at least. Technically, one of the good guys did the real damage. A nasty little bitch named Rail Blade. But she's either dead or in a secret prison, rotting away. She's been missing as long as we have."

Pit sat on the edge of his bed. "So. We were bad guys."

"We were revolutionaries. We were fighting for a cause."

"We should have stuck to robbing banks."

"I've never robbed a bank in my life," said Sunday. She was a little offended by the suggestion. She was a soldier, not a thief.

"Don't sound so judgmental," said Pit. "I've been robbing convenience stores the last month while waiting for you to show up. It's practically honest work compared to blowing up cities."

Sunday sighed. "Maybe I shouldn't be so close-minded. When dad disappeared, I went to live on his yacht in the Bahamas. He had two million in cash in the safe. But . . . it's been years, and I'm down to my last thousand bucks. I was really hoping the box would be filled with hundred dollar bills." She picked up the gun. "What the hell am I supposed to do with this thing?"

"The letter said it was for your leg."

"Not quite."

"It's a regeneration ray. What else are you supposed to use it for?"

"I'm not shooting myself with some mystery ray gun that turned up in the mail. What if it's a trap by one of our enemies to neutralize our power?"

"Use it on me," said Pit.

She eyed his face. She raised the gun. For a moment, she hesitated. What if this was a trap? Would she blow his brains out with this thing? She'd killed a lot of people, but could she really shoot the one person left on earth who was kind of, just a little bit, her friend? She closed her eyes and pulled the trigger.

The gun spoke. "DNA analysis commencing."

She opened her eyes. A tight green laser beam formed a dot in the middle of Pit Geek's brow. "Analysis finished. Calculating age." Now a blue dot appeared on his forehead. "Analysis inconclusive. The median male age of 35.5 will be approximated. Beginning tissue deconstruction."

Then, exactly the thing that Sunday had feared came true. Pit Geek's face simply vaporized, revealing mangled bones beneath. She held her aim steady as the gun continued to speak. "Repairing underlying structures." One by one, the bones of his skull began to shift and crawl back into alignment. His gray, gnarled teeth faded out one by one into mists of static, only to reform an instant later as healthy white enamel. "Underlying structures repaired. Commencing tissue reconstruction."

The effect was very much like something from Star Trek. The air in front of Pit Geek's skull began to shimmer with bright yellow sparkles. Then a ghostly face appeared over his restored bones, gradually growing more and more dense, until suddenly Pit Geek was whole once more. He blinked as the gun said, "Regeneration complete."

"Holy shit," said Sunday. "It worked."

"Did it?" said Pit, feeling his face. "I don't feel different. Still can't remember more than little fragments."

"It fixed your face, not your brain," said Sunday. "I think it read your DNA, figured out what you were supposed to look like, then built you a new face. I don't think memories could be fixed by giving you a new brain. In fact, it would probably wipe them out."

Pit Geek stood up and went to the mirror.

"Who the hell. . . ?" he mumbled. His jaw went slack. He raised his hand to touch his scalp, which was now covered in thick dark curls. He ran his finger along the line where his face hadn't quite meshed up before. The skin was smooth, free of wrinkles. The DNA reset had left him with eyebrows, but had rebuilt the rest of his face without even the hint of a five o'clock shadow.

"I look like a movie star," he said, his voice distant.

Sunday wouldn't go that far. His eyes were still kind of beady, and his nose was slightly too big. But the ray had taken at least twenty years off his face. Not to mention at least a quarter inch of grime.

He must have been noticing the same thing. "Aw hell," he

said. "I gotta start washing my face now. It's like having a new car. You gotta wash it every week."

"Some people wash their face every day, you know."

He chuckled. "Ma'am, that ain't the cowboy way."

"You were a cowboy?" she asked.

He frowned. "Was I a cowboy?" Then he turned to her. "Take off your pants. Let's fix your leg."

She stood, pausing for a second as she fumbled with her belt. Why was she hesitant? She used to burn her clothes off all the time as Sundancer. Pit Geek had seen her naked a hundred times or more. But, before, he'd just been this dirty zombie coot with the unexplained ability to swallow anything. Until this moment, she'd never thought of him as a man. Like, a *man* man, who might find pleasure in seeing her with no clothes.

Sunday frowned. Where was this bourgeoisie modesty suddenly coming from? She'd shaken off the last remnants of those old values long, long ago. Letting out her breath, she dropped her pants.

She looked toward him. "Are you leering at me?"

He shrugged. "You've filled out since I last saw you."

"Are you saying I'm fat?"

"No! Hell no. You're a damn fine looking woman. With hips like those, you could be a high dollar whore. I can't wait to see you with both legs."

She sat on the edge of the bed and removed her c-leg.

"You know I lost my leg because of a hand grenade you threw, right?" she asked. "You still owe me."

"Wah, wah, wah," said Pit Geek. "You lost a leg. I came out of that battle as a head in a cooler. We both got our sob stories."

Perhaps it was Sunday's imagination, but Pit seemed . . . feistier than he had five minutes ago. Maybe the ray *had* affected his brain? Or maybe having a good looking face was making him cocky?

"Okay," she said. "Do it."

So he did it. The laser ran along the stub of her limb just below the knee. The machine ran through the same pattern as before. It correctly pegged her age as twenty five. When the underlying structures were rebuilt, she watched with fascination as bones began to materialize from thin air. She wondered where the calcium to build them was coming from. With Pit Geek, matter had simply been rearranged. Here, something new was being built. Was it her imagination, or was her whole body tingling? Was the ray stealing material from the rest of her? But she had no time to ponder. As the flesh and muscles faded back into their proper place, waves of pain rushed through her as the newly formed nerves knitted themselves back into her nervous system. The pain made her vision blur and left a metallic taste in her mouth.

Then the pain was gone, and she had a new leg. Like Pit's face, the leg was hairless. She frowned. It didn't match her other leg at all.

"Did it think I was white?" she asked, staring at the almost milky hue of her new limb.

"Ah, you just need a tan," said Pit Geek. "It looks a hell of a lot better than that bionic woman crap you were hopping around on. Be happy."

"A: I wasn't hopping. Most people didn't even notice the leg was artificial. B: I don't really do happy. Happy is for people who aren't trying to save the planet. I can't be happy while we're at war."

"We aren't at war. The boss says it's over."

"But we haven't won!" Sunday clenched her fists tightly.

"Ain't we? You seen the headlines lately? The US has about bankrupted itself fighting wars all over the place. Some people are saying it's the next Great Depression. They talk like the world's right on the edge of falling apart."

"If it's on the edge, we should push it," said Sunday.

"Or . . . hear me out here . . . or we could just rob some banks."

"What is it with you and banks?" she asked, shaking her heads.

"How can you not know this?" said Pit. "Banks are where the money's at."

Sunday stared at her new foot. In addition to a tan, what it really, really needed was a nice pair of shoes.

"Okay," she said. "Let's try things your way for a change. Let's rob some banks."

Pit Geek held the gun toward an imaginary bank teller. "Hand over the money!" he said, then chuckled. "Man, this thing will scare the pants off of folks."

Sunday giggled, a sound she hadn't made in several years.

"Did you just laugh?" Pit Geek sounded astonished.

She shrugged. "Just, well, what you said struck me as funny, considering I'm sitting here in my panties."

"So you are," said Pit, stepping toward her bed.

She lifted a glowing finger. "I hope you remember that I can vaporize flesh."

"So you can," said Pit, dropping onto the other bed. "Man. Robbing banks. Just like the old days."

"We never robbed banks in the old days," said Sunday.

Pit went silent as he stared at the ceiling. "I'm pretty sure we did it on horseback," he whispered.

Things I don't remember eating:
The Coke machine.
The 1969 Yellow Pages for Dallas.
Two cans of purple paint.
A peacock feather boa.
What looks like it might be part of an
industrial sized air-conditioner.
The front end of a Dodge Dart.
An actual set of darts, plus the
dartboard they were stuck in.
A TV cart.
What might be but almost certainly isn't
the real Mona Lisa.
A five-gallon gasoline can, empty.
Airline peanuts, still in the bag.
An ugly necktie, about five inches wide,
kind of a snot green with stripes the
color of Grape Nehi.
A penguin. It's dead now. My guess is,
it starved. The chickens here eat the
bugs in the trash and the goats seem to
hang on eating the garbage directly. I
guess I didn't eat much in the way of
penguin food.
A set of three by five note cards, about
a dozen of them, with writing in what
might be Russian. It's got those
backwards R's and a half dozen other
letters I can't cipher. Or maybe it's my
handwriting, from back in the years when
I had a pound of shrapnel churning up my
gray matter.
Oh Sunday. Things were so much simpler
when I was dumb.

Chapter Four
Not Bonny, Not Clyde

THEIR FIRST BANK was a SunTrust central branch in downtown Richmond. It was crowded, lunch hour, when a lot of people rushed in to take care of business. Pit had thought they should start smaller and with fewer witnesses, but Sunday had been adamant that they should do this big. She said she wanted a bank robbery so spectacular people would talk about it in China. Pit had gotten swept along in her enthusiasm. Spectacular was now the plan.

So, step one was to drive a motorcycle right into the bank's lobby. If Monday had been around, his space machine would have been the right tool for the job, but the morning after they'd used the Regeneration Ray they'd left the motel office to find this beautiful Harley parked next to the Camry. They took it as a sign that their crime spree should begin with a little grand theft. They needed some kind of transportation since Sunday was graceful as an angel when she was in flight by herself, but if she carried anything heavier than a watermelon she usually lost her center of balance and spiraled down to crash landings. Thus, a getaway vehicle was a necessity.

Pit gunned the bike up the plaza steps in front of the bank. The building had a series of concrete posts near the doors designed to stop people from driving a large vehicle into the building, but the Harley slipped right through. Crashing into the plate glass windows might have damaged the bike, so at the last second Sunday stretched her arm out, wiggled her fingers, and BOOM no more window. They skid to a halt amid flaming debris and about a hundred screaming customers.

They had moments before cops showed up, not that either of

them was worried about cops. When Sunday really lit up, bullets disintegrated before touching her. Pit wasn't scared of bullets, and was scared even less now that they had a Regeneration Ray.

Despite the fact that the sky was filled with gray clouds and it felt cold enough to snow, this was a fine, fine day to be a supervillain.

The first order of business was the rent-a-cop stationed near the door. His face was red as a beet as he ran toward them, drawing his pistol. He aimed it toward them with trembling arms and shouted, "Put your hands up!"

Which they did, but only to take off their helmets. They both dismounted the bike, smiling at the guard.

"Put that thing down before you hurt yourself," said Pit. Then he turned to the rest of the room and shouted, "Everyone on the floor, please! We'll be done robbing this joint in five minutes and y'all can get back to your lives."

"Put your hands up!" the guard repeated, shouting louder. "Put your hands up!"

Pit sighed. "What are you, a broken record?"

Sunday began to undress as Pit walked toward the guard. Under her biker's jacket she was wearing a leather halter top and blue jeans that looked painted on. She'd spent the seven longest hours of Pit Geek's life shopping for these jeans and the calf-high zipper boots that went over them, and she wasn't planning to just blow these things to atoms the first time she wore them in public.

Pit felt a little sorry for the guard. Sorry for himself a little too. They both would have preferred to watch the strip show, but instead their eyes were locked on one another. Pit approached with his palms open. The guard probably wouldn't fire at an unarmed man.

The guard shot him in the chest from a yard away. When Pit didn't fall, he shot him again, and again, until his clip was empty.

Pit snatched the empty gun away. "First nice clothes I've worn in months and you had to go put holes in them," he grumbled.

He was decked out in biker's leathers, even leather pants. Secretly, he was happy that the jacket now had a nice pattern of holes. He'd felt a little dainty wearing clothes without even a scuff mark.

Pit pointed the gun at the guard. "Now you get on the floor." The guard looked confused. "The . . . the gun's empty," he said.

"So it is," said Pit. "I knew that." He frowned. "Well, I'm in luck, because my doctor told me I have an iron deficiency." Then, in three neat gulps, he ate the gun. He could have downed it in one bite, but it wouldn't have had the same impact. The guard's eyes looked like they were going to pop out of his skull.

"Down," said Pit.

The guard went down.

Pit looked back and found that Sunday had finished stripping. Unfortunately, she was already sheathed in white radiance that forced him to shield his eyes. She walked toward the row of tellers, leaving a line of flaming footprints. As she neared the first customer lying on the floor, she climbed into the air like she was walking up invisible steps. There were red velvet ropes forming a little maze for customers to traipse through. They caught fire as she walked over them. She descended on the other side of the tellers, in front of the steel vault door. She walked into the door as if it wasn't even there, because, by the time she reached it, it wasn't. At her hottest, she could vaporize steel. Fortunately, in the ten years Pit had known her she'd honed her powers so that she could direct her full body blasts in a single direction, or else everyone behind her would now be dead.

Pit ran toward the wall of tellers and vaulted behind the counter. He could now hear distant sirens. He shouted to the room, "Everybody just stay calm and stay down! Sounds like help is on the way. No need for anyone here to be a hero."

He ducked to slip into the bank vault. The Sunday-sized hole in the door was a good six inches shorter than he was. Inside, Sunday was already vaporizing locks on safe deposit boxes and yanking them open. Gold coins, jewelry, and comic books in polybags were being tossed into a pile. Legal papers were reduced to ash.

Pit sucked down the valuables. Then he turned his attention to all the cash, shoving stacks of hundreds, fifties, and twenties between his teeth. It took several minutes to finish off the vault. Pit wasn't good enough at math to have a real guess of how much he'd just swallowed. Certainly at least a million.

They went back into the lobby.

"You guys are doing fine," Pit said. "Give us two more minutes and you can all whip out your phones and tell folks how you were just robbed by the modern Bonnie and Clyde."

Sunday turned her head sharply towards him, in what might have been a nasty look, though with her face too bright to focus on it was tough to say.

She said to the room, "When you get on your phones, you tell people that no bank in the world is safe. Not just from us: the so called authorities of this world create a theatre of safety to make you feel as if your money is secure, while all the time they steal you blind. The safest place for your money is in your mattress. Tell people!"

"What the hell was that about?" Pit asked as they reached the motorcycle. "That wasn't in the script."

"I was unaware there was a script," she said.

"Not a real script, but, y'know, there's a flow to these things."

"I've never gone with the flow," she said, moving on.

Sunday had folded up her clothes as she undressed and placed them neatly in the saddlebags. Pit secured Sunday's helmet to the back seat as she floated out to the plaza, the glass windows melting like ice at her approach.

Pit straddled the bike as gunfire erupted outside.

"Y'all keep your heads down, y'hear?" he said to the customers on the floor. "It's been a nice, clean robbery so far. Hate to see any of you kind folks get perforated by a stray bullet."

Then he gunned the motor and roared out onto the plaza. He skidded to a halt to watch the action. He felt rather heroic, standing in front of a smoking bank with a hail of bullets flying around him. Of course, none of the bullets were aimed at him. The flying woman sheathed in white flames had a lock on the cop's attention at this point.

"No one is safe!" Sunday shouted from overhead. He stretched her arms toward the first cop car. It exploded, taking out the cops next to it. She pointed toward the second car. These cops were fast learners and started running. Two seconds later the car went off like a bomb. Smoking bits of twisted steel clattered on the cement plaza like a shower of hail.

There were four more cop cars and four more booms. Any remaining officers had retreated behind a freshly arrived fire truck.

The firemen hastily hooked a hose to a hydrant. Sunday crossed her arms as she waited for them to finish.

She glanced down at Pit. "See you in Short Pump."

Pit nodded, then put on his helmet.

The jet of water shot toward Sunday. And then there was steam, vast, billowing clouds of white vapor that rolled across the plaza and quickly reduced the line of sight for the surrounding blocks to about three feet. Pit wheeled out ahead of the billowing cloud, darting through traffic stalled by the police action. There was a helicopter overhead, but only for a moment. A second sun flashed through the sky near the chopper and it began to spin out of control.

They met up behind an old vacant K-Mart in Short Pump. Sunday made Pit turn his back as she dressed.

"We're not Bonny, not Clyde," she complained as she pulled on her boots. "Where did that come from?"

"What's your problem with Bonny and Clyde?"

"To start with, they were lovers," she said. "I don't want the world to think we're sleeping together."

"Why the hell not?" Pit asked. "You don't mind being known as a terrorist, but you're worried people might think you're loose?"

Sunday pressed her lips tightly together. Then she said, "In any case, it's unoriginal. We aren't copying anybody. We're originals. Pit Geek and Sundancer."

"I don't want to be Pit Geek no more," said Pit.

"What do you mean?"

He shrugged. "I got a new face. I got some nice clean clothes. Maybe I don't want people to know I used to live in a pit and bite the heads off chickens."

"I have a feeling that, face or no face, people are going to put two and two together. Pit Geek could shrug off bullets and eat solid steel. On the debut of your new face, you shrugged off bullets and ate a pistol. I've got a hunch someone is going to make the connection, Pit."

"Devourer," said Pit Geek.

"That's your new name? Devourer?"

"It's more dignified."

"I don't like it. It doesn't roll off the tongue. It has two soft 'R' sounds mushed together."

"Eater?" Pit said.

"Pithier, but I don't think it's that much more dignified than Pit Geek. People reading about you in the newspaper will think you have a weight problem."

"You should go back to Burn Baby."

"No," said Sunday. "And it was Baby Burn. And what's wrong with Sundancer?"

"You're the one who wants to be original. Any time I hear Sundancer, I think of the Sundance Kid. People will start thinking I'm Butch Cassidy."

"I've heard of the movie," said Sunday.

"There was a movie?" asked Pit.

"That's where Butch Cassidy and the Sundance Kid come from," said Sunday.

"Naw, they were real people," said Pit. "Butch had a gang that used to rob trains and banks. The Wild Bunch. Sundance was part of the gang. His real name was . . . was Harry. Harry, uh, Harry Longbow? Anyway, he stole a horse from a ranch in Sundance was how he got his name."

Sunday gave him a puzzled look. "You can't remember your own name, but you know the name of some fictional cowboy?"

"He ain't fictional."

"Whatever," said Sunday. "I'm vetoing Baby Burn right now. Burn Baby also. You can call yourself Toiletman for all I care."

"Toiletman?"

"Since you shove crap down a hole," she said, sounding as if it should have been obvious.

"Speaking of crap, what was that bit about putting money into mattresses? We want it in banks so we can steal it."

"You want to steal it. I don't see much point in us acquiring a lot of wealth. But I do think that, as you said, the whole world's on edge right now. The planet's already suffering economic turmoil. If we trigger a run on banks, we might bring down the house of cards. Money only has value because people think it has value. Destroy the underlying belief system, and you destroy money. Destroy money, and civilization crumbles."

Pit nodded slowly. "Um-hmm. And, just so I'm clear, why, exactly, do we want to destroy civilization?"

She rolled her eyes. "Didn't you pick up anything from your time with Monday?"

Pit shrugged. "If I did, it got blasted out at some point."

"Civilization was once a great evolutionary innovation. It elevated mankind above the animals. But, sadly, civilization has now become a destructive force."

"Like pollution?" asked Pit.

"I mean it's destroying mankind. Nature's law requires that the fittest survive if a species is to thrive. But powerful men have co-opted civilization to ensure that the strongest members of the species are thrown into prisons. They pay the most dimwitted and weak to stay at home and breed generation after generation of imbeciles. Civilization has become a tool of devolution, returning men to the state of animals, where the whole goal of life is to consume and breed as little more than two legged cattle."

"Why would they do that?" Pit scratched the back of his neck. "And who are they, for that matter?"

Sunday shrugged. "I can't say if the harm inflicted was by accident or by design. But the only hope for man to return to the evolutionary fires where he can be forged into something stronger is to wipe out this poisonous culture. One day, future men will thank us for destroying the value of money."

Pit patted his belly. "Could you maybe wait until we spent this million bucks before you destroy civilization?"

"That was a lot more than a million that you wolfed down," said Sunday. "But so what? Where the hell are we supposed to be spending it? I mean, I have to lay out some dough each year to keep the yacht fueled so the generators can keep the place air conditioned, but it's not like I can take the boat anywhere. Dad's bribed the local officials into thinking I'm a mafia informant under witness protection by the FBI. But I can't take the boat to another country, because I don't think the faked paperwork would stand up to scrutiny. And, anyway, why do I need a boat? I can fly!"

"Yeah, buck naked. You could show up places wearing clothes if you had a boat."

Sunday gave a grim smile as she nodded.

"What do we need money for?" she asked, not looking at him directly. She was staring off in the distance, thinking out loud. "We can't buy a house with it. Cars? If we want an expensive car, we can just steal it. Diamonds? We can rob a jewelry store just as easily as a bank. Anyway, who wants jewelry? What's it good for?"

"Most women like jewelry."

"Most women like being given jewelry," said Sunday. "Our warped society has taught them that they only have worth if they have a diamond on their finger. All sexual relationships are tainted by this thinly disguised variant of prostitution."

"So you wouldn't sleep with me if I gave you a diamond ring?"

"Nope."

"How about if I make a solemn vow not to give you a diamond ring?"

"Definitely not."

"What if I were a woman?"

"What kind of stupid question is that?"

Pit shrugged. "You've just never shown any interest in men."

"And that makes me a lesbian?" Sunday rolled her eyes. "The day I met Rex Monday, I knew that I'd never have a relationship with a man. He opened up my mind to the truths of the world, things I'd always seen, but never had the courage to accept."

"Like what?"

"Like I'm not human. I'm the next step up the evolutionary chain, the first of my kind. I need to kick start evolution so I won't be the last. Sleeping with an ordinary man . . . it's like you sleeping with a monkey." She gave him a sideways glance. "You, uh, wouldn't do that, would you?"

"Naw," said Pit. There was a pause. Then he added, "I'd eat one, though."

"I'm sure you would."

There was another moment of silence.

"So," Pit said. "I, uh, I might be another step up the evolutionary chain as well."

"Maybe," said Sunday. "But you don't brush your teeth. You make it easy to say no."

Pit nodded slowly. He turned his head and furtively slipped a finger between his lips, running it along his new chompers. They didn't feel dirty.

"So," he said. "What if I—"

"Give up, Pit."

"Whatever. What next?" he asked, getting back on the bike.

"We go find some hotel in the sticks and watch TV. See if the world collapses. If it doesn't, we rob a bigger bank. Hell, we'll take out Fort Knox if we have too."

"But that's all we're spending the money on? Hotel rooms?"

She shrugged as she got on the bike behind him. "What's your idea?"

"Step one, we go buy us some more nice duds, then find a saloon where we can get plastered and dance the night away."

"I don't drink or dance."

"You don't dance?" Pit said, starting the engine. "It's right in your name!"

53

"I picked that name when I was fifteen. I . . . lord, this sounds silly. I'd been taking ballet since I was a little girl. I really wasn't good at it, but at fifteen I still thought I'd be a ballerina."

"I don't think that sounds silly. Girls like that stuff."

"Only because we're brainwashed by a culture of subservience. I can see now how sick it is that people trot out their prepubescent daughters in tights and tutus to advertise their sexual desirability. The world is just one horrible ongoing nightmare once you truly wake up inside it."

"I don't know about all that," said Pit, gliding the bike forward around the speed bumps beside the K-Mart. "I just know it's fun to do the two-step with Merle Haggard spinning on the juke box."

"What's step two?" she asked.

"The two-step is a dance," said Pit.

"No. I know that. I said what's step two? You started your idea with, 'step one.'"

"Right," said Pit. "I was thinking about monkeys 'cause of what you said. And, you know, there is one place we can go to spend our dough and live like kings."

"Pangea?"

"Monkeyland!" Pit nodded. "The law couldn't touch us!"

"The whole place is made of garbage!" Sunday said.

"Garbage might start to look valuable if you kill off the dollar," Pit said with a laugh, though she might not have heard him since that was the instant he gunned the motor and they roared back onto the highway. Sunday wrapped her arms tightly around him, her breasts pressed up against his back, the cheek of her helmet pushed against his shoulder blade.

The gray skies began to drizzle. The wind howled as if it were in pain as the bike knifed through the air. Sunday let loose just enough heat to warm them.

It was a fine morning to be a supervillain.

It's quiet here. Occasionally, I hear a goat or a chicken off in the distance, but normally it's silent as a tomb. There was a time in my life when I wanted a little peace and quiet.

Be careful what you wish for.

Chapter Five
The Covenant

THE SUPERMEN arrived via private jet at Guantanamo Bay. Sarah was at the controls, Clint was seated next to her, and Johnny was in the back staring out the window at the blue sea below as they drew closer to the base. The sea changed to a lighter hue as they neared land. The sun was behind them, casting the shadow of the plane on the giant plastic dome that covered the base.

Guantanamo was where they kept captured aliens, as well as human terrorists considered too dangerous for ordinary prisons. Johnny watched Sarah closely as she guided the plane. Nothing about her body language indicated she was worried they were heading for a trap. She had a lot more experience in these situations, even though she was technically only a few years older than Johnny. But Johnny had spent most of the last decade as a dematerialized cluster of fundamental particles, which meant he was effectively a good deal younger than the date on his birth certificate would suggest.

The sunlight dimmed as they glided through the jet gate of the dome. All of Johnny's data streams in his retinal display died off instantly. They were now cut off from radio contact with the outside world. If they were headed into a trap, they would have no way of calling for help.

They disembarked on the runway surrounded by acres of featureless beige sand. The air was cool, dank and stale, with a faint tone of bleach reminding Johnny of the smell of his first boyfriend's basement apartment. The dome recycled all its air to keep any alien contagions inside, though Simpson back at the base had assured him that alien germs were utterly harmless, since they hadn't evolved to infect human cells.

They were met by a jeep that carried them to General Shepard's residence. Johnny had expected fancier digs, but the Shepard made his home in the same kind of one-story tin-roofed shack that the rest of the base was composed off. His house was walled off with twelve-foot-tall chain-link fences topped with razor wire. Johnny counted at least thirty cameras pointed at the structure. If he hadn't known better, he would have assumed the place was built to keep the general a prisoner.

The interior was as gray and Spartan as the exterior. Piles of money were being thrown into the defense of earth from aliens and terrorists, but apparently the money wasn't landing here. They were taken to a conference room with a long metal table and folding chairs. There was a calendar on the wall, with the November photo showing a kitten staring at a turkey.

Johnny and Sarah took a seat. Clint remained standing, his arms crossed. He stared at the gray metal table.

"It looks like a good place to strap down a prisoner for interrogation," he said.

"This isn't a trap," Sarah said. She still had her helmet on. It resembled a motorcycle helmet with a mirrored visor and hid her face completely. Her plastic surgery made it safe for her to move around in public now, but she still needed the voice modulators. This conversation was no doubt going to be recorded. If the government found a match with a previous recording of Sarah, it would be game over.

The door opened. General Shepard came into the room alone. He was a man in his sixties, with a comb-over of about a dozen gray hairs. The leathery skin of his face seemed to have come detached from his skull, reminding Johnny of a basset hound.

Shepard cleared his throat. "Let me cut straight to the most important thing for you to keep in mind during this meeting. Public use of meta-human powers has been an official act of terrorism for seven years now. If any of you try anything, I have a patriotic duty to lock you into cells for the rest of your lives."

"Nice to meet you too," Clint said, gruffly.

"Yes," said Sarah, in a warmer tone. "It's nice to meet you, sir.

We recognize that our presence here creates a difficult situation for you. We appreciate your willingness to listen to our proposal."

The general took a seat. "Let's hear it."

"We're the first to admit that the world has gotten along fine without superheroes for the last seven years," said Sarah. "That's changed with the return of Sundancer and Pit Geek. If supervillains are back, you need us on your side."

"Ma'am, I think you underestimate the advances we've made in the last couple of years in the field of meta-human controls."

Sarah nodded. "I'm sure you have some impressive toys, but the undeniable fact is that you haven't caught them yet. They've hit five banks in ten days, and now that footage of Sundancer's little speeches were captured on a cell phone and placed on You-Tube, the runs on banks have gotten out of hand. When Bank of America closed its branches early in Atlanta yesterday, it set off riots. Today was the fourth day in a row the stock market has fallen over five percent. If Sundancer and Pit Geek continue their crime spree another ten days, we could face total economic collapse."

Shepard stared at Sarah as she made her case. He said nothing when she finished, but turned his gaze to study them one by one. Johnny's palms grew sweaty.

Finally, Shepard asked, "What makes you think you can find them?"

"We don't need to find them. We just need to respond to their next robbery in time to catch them."

"Is that all?" Shepard grumbled. "For all our analysts can figure out, they might be picking targets by throwing darts at a map. How can you know what city to be in before they strike again?"

"It doesn't matter," said Sarah. "We have access to technology that will allow us to respond instantly the second that another sighting is made."

Shepard drummed his fingers on the table as he contemplated these words. "Then it's true. Katrina Knowbokov has Rex Monday's space machine. You know possessing that technology is illegal."

"In the U.S. Not where we're keeping it."

"The space machine is the most dangerous weapon ever created," said Shepard. "In theory, a terrorist could simply cut and paste a whole city into the sun."

Sarah shook her head. "If that were possible, don't you think Rex Monday would have done it? The machine isn't magic. It takes energy to operate. Moving a single human around the globe is a costly process. I assure you, cities are safe."

"Fine. But you could still toss the president into the sun if you wanted to."

"Snatching a remote target is next to impossible unless it's been laced with tracer nanites. Otherwise, we'd already have Pit Geek and Sundancer in custody."

Shepard crossed his arms and gave Sarah a skeptical look. "Let's pretend you haven't just confessed to possessing illegal technology. I'll also pretend that I don't know who you really are. You've come here to make a case that you're the right people for the crisis at hand. Make it. Who are you, and what can you do?"

"Skyrider," said Sarah. "I can fly and neutralize the gravity of anything I touch, giving me super-strength. My flight uniform is Kevlar with an energy dampening mesh beneath it. I'm not invulnerable, but I can take most things that are thrown at me."

Sarah's flight uniform was sky blue with navy blue trim. It clung to her curvy body like a glove. Her helmet was the darker blue. She didn't have an inch of exposed skin. With her voice modulator, she sounded suspiciously robotic. "My real name is Sarah Sandlin," she continued. "Our contact has provided your people with the documentation you need to confirm out identities. Unlike previous superheroes, we've nothing to hide. We want to work with authorities instead of taking the law into our own hands. We call ourselves the Covenant. We intend to be heroes the world can trust."

Shepard looked toward Clint. Clint was a big man, built like a linebacker. Save for his logo, his uniform was all white, so bright and pure it hurt to stare at it. On the center of his chest there was a large red "S."

"Clint Christianson," Clint said. "My code name is Servant. My body generates force fields that produce various effects. I'm completely invulnerable. I don't need to breathe. I can run two hundred miles an hour by compressing the time dimension caught within my fields. I can bend steel with my bare hands."

"You fly?" asked Shepard.

"Not really. I can jump about a quarter mile."

Shepard turned to Johnny. "Son, you're a little young for this game."

Johnny shook his head. "Name's Johnny Appleton. The birth certificate we sent in should show you I'm twenty seven." Of course, ten of those years he hadn't aged. Biologically, he was only seventeen.

"Code name?" asked Shepard.

"Call me Ap," said Johnny. "I'm the world's first open source superhero. Ten years ago, Rex Monday was trying to design a teleportation belt. He needed a guinea pig, so he had his henchmen kidnap some random victim off the street. Lucky me, I'm the guy they snatched. Monday strapped the belt on me, fiddled with the dials, and tore me down to a cloud of quantum particles. Unfortunately, the supercomputer he was using to piece me back together wasn't up to the task. I was stuck in a dematerialized state until a few months ago, when the Katrina Knowbokov Foundation rescued me."

The Foundation was an independent team of the world's best scientists who'd been assembled to make sense of the mad-scientist inventions of Rex Monday and Dr. Nicholas Knowbokov, both now deceased. The team had been able to put Johnny back together, but his years in a diffuse quantum state had left his atomic structure highly unstable. The belt now essentially was constantly rematerializing him in order to keep him from fading back into nothingness.

One side effect of his instability was that by making minor programming alterations to the belt, he could change his body. The scientists at the foundation had written a few superpowers for him, sort of as a consolation prize for his missing years.

Johnny had since published the belt's code on the internet. Now, thousands of programmers around the world uploaded new programs daily for him to test. He now had thousands of different powers, and since his old life was pretty much over he'd lobbied to join the Covenant. He wanted to make the world a safer place than it had been for him growing up.

Shepard leaned back in his chair. His cheeks swayed as he shook his head sadly. "For a team making a pact to be open and honest, you're getting off to a damn shitty start."

"How so?" Johnny asked.

"First off all, you check out," said Shepard. "You've given us your real name and verifiable contact information. But nowhere in this information did you tell us anything about your criminal record."

Johnny rolled his eyes. "What?" he said. "Just because I'm black you think I have a criminal record?"

"I think you have a criminal record because I've read it," said Shepard.

Johnny felt the blood drain from his face. "I was a juvenile. Those records are sealed."

"I unsealed them," said Shepard. "You've been arrested for prostitution, what, seven times?"

Johnny's mouth went dry.

"You started smoking crack when you were sixteen," said Shepard. "Dropped out of school. Ran away from home a few weeks after that. First actual arrest for solicitation was in San Diego six months later. Then, pretty much once every other week until Monday's men grabbed you."

Johnny let out his breath slowly. He was determined not to lose his temper. "I understand you may feel the need to judge me," he said. "But I haven't used drugs in over a decade. When the team put me back together, I was clean. I've been given a new lease on life. I don't need artificial substances to make me feel good about myself."

"Very inspirational," said Shepard. "But if I authorize the Covenant to operate openly, how long do you think it will take others to discover your past? How much of a hero are you going to be once the National Enquirer tracks down some of your old clients for their opinions of you?"

"If it happens, I'll deal with it," said Johnny.

Shepard turned to Clint. "Your birth certificate checks out. So, we checked out your contacts. They also passed."

"I've got nothing to hide," said Clint.

"Don't you?" asked Shepard. "Because you've got the same biometric energy signature as a super-powered drug lord that used to operate out of Detroit. Called himself Ogre. He ran the seedier parts of that town like a two-bit king, until Rail Blade sealed him in a cube of solid steel thirty feet on each side."

"I didn't really keep up with the news back then," said Clint.

Shepard shifted his gaze toward Sarah. "You barely even tried, girl. Sarah Sandlin? You're Sarah Knowbokov, the Thrill. You played a role in the destruction of Jerusalem. You're just as much a fugitive as Sundancer."

Sarah shrugged. "An interesting theory."

"No, it's an interesting fact," said Shepard. "The other interesting fact is that your mother is Katrina Knowbokov, and since she inherited all your father's patents, she's the richest woman in the world. If she hadn't backed the purchase of nine trillion dollars in debt in US and European bonds this week, the entire financial system might have collapsed."

"Yes," said Sarah. "It might have."

"That kind of money buys a lot of second chances," said Shepard. "Whoever you are."

"We are who we appear to be," said Sarah. "We're three people who want to help save the world."

"I got a call from the President this morning. Apparently Mrs. Knowbokov called to discuss the possibility of further bond purchases, and the subject of the swift authorization of your activities came up. Not that there is any quid pro quo."

"Of course not," said Sarah.

Shepard once again drummed his fingers on the table. "So. How do I reach you? Some kind of fancy laser that paints a big 'C' on the moon?"

"I've got a cell phone in my helmet," said Sarah. "Ap has one in his belt. We'll give you both numbers."

Shepard eyed Clint. "Why don't you have one?"

Clint shrugged. "No pockets."

"He's the strong and silent type anyway," said Sarah. "Johnny and I handle the talking."

"Nope," said Shepard. "Before I turn you loose on Sundancer and Pit Geek, there's going to be a press conference. If we play it right, just announcing that we have three meta-humans working on our side is going to reverse some of the damage these two have inflicted on the financial markets. For maximum positive press, Servant will be your spokesman."

"I don't like public speaking," said Servant.

Sarah said, "And I'm completely comfortable—"

Shepard cut her off. "You're hiding your face and your voice is plainly altered. It's hard to sell the idea that your team has nothing to hide if the spokesman is so blatantly hiding something."

"Then I'll handle the media," said Johnny. Like Clint, he wore no mask. His costume was a set of red tights with a large 'A' on the chest, with black gloves and boots to match the black teleporter belt. Between the three costumes, they were red, white, and blue. It wasn't the most subtle appeal to gain people's trust.

Shepard shook his head. "No offense son, but even if I hadn't read your record, the first time I heard you speak I knew you were queer as a three dollar bill."

Johnny felt like he'd been slapped.

Sarah jumped in, "Sir, I hardly think Johnny's sexuality will be an issue."

"You're nuts," said Shepard. "And, even if he was straight, he's still a damn teenager, and practically a midget."

"Now you're just being gratuitously offensive," said Sarah.

"It's okay," said Johnny, determined not to sound flustered. He was five six, just two inches shorter than the average male height. He only looked short because he was in the same room as Clint. "I've been called worse."

Shepard turned to Servant. "Like it or not, you look like a

hero, and you've got a hero's voice. James Earl Jones would be envious. You're the spokesman."

Clint shrugged. "Fine."

"The first question the press will ask is, are you Ogre?"

"No."

"One word answers won't do."

"No, sir."

"Then where did you get your powers?"

"From the Lord," said Servant.

The general stared at him.

"I became Servant after accepting Jesus Christ as my lord and savior." Johnny had never heard Clint's origin story before, and at first thought the big man was joking, but as he continued talking Johnny thought he sounded utterly sincere. "God gave me these powers to use for the good of all mankind. As long as I have my faith, I'll have my powers."

The general grinned. "Oh, the folks in fly-over country are going to love this."

THINGS TURNED UGLY when they got back on the plane.

"The nerve of that bastard," Johnny grumbled. "Acts like I'm an embarrassment because I'm gay."

Clint shook his head. "You should have told us."

"You didn't know he was gay?" Sarah asked, with a tone of surprise that Johnny found bothersome.

"So he's got a funny voice," said Clint. "I try not to judge people."

"What's funny about my voice?" said Johnny.

"Never mind," said Clint. "Anyway, what I meant was, you should have told us about your record. The Covenant is supposed to represent the highest moral standards. It's hard to think of anything less moral than having a faggot prostitute on our team."

"I thought you were Christian," said Johnny, crossing his arms. "You're not being very love-your-neighbor at the moment."

"Loving my neighbor means trying to help that neighbor get

into heaven," Clint said. "If you're having sex with men, that's a sin. I know people who can help get you straight."

"Get me straight? It's not a disease. It's just how I was born."

"Maybe you could use the belt to fix it," said Clint.

"It's not something that needs fixing!"

"Guys, let's just calm down," said Sarah, as the plane taxied down the runway. "We've got a long flight home."

"So," said Johnny. "Were you Ogre? Because being a murderous drug lord trumps being a hungry teenager who had to do some unpleasant things in order to buy a meal."

"You could've walked into any church in San Diego and asked for help," said Clint.

"You didn't answer my question."

"Who I used to be doesn't matter," said Clint. "I've been born again. I'm a new man."

"Then you were Ogre."

Clint shook his head. "There's a solid steel cube in Detroit you could cut open if you ever wanted to find out the truth."

"Or you could tell me the truth."

"I'm Clint Christenson. I'm Servant. This is truth."

Things went quiet after that. Clint stared out the window as they cleared the dome. Sarah looked straight ahead. Johnny pulled the wireless keypad off his belt and activated his retinal display. He'd been off-line for almost two hours. In the missing time he'd gotten two hundred comments on Facebook on his proposed costume changes. People were enthusiastic about swapping the white capital "A" for the "@" symbol.

Of course, there was also the usual trove of spam. "What a fag costume!" someone named Alpha Dude had posted. Johnny started to delete the comment, but left it. Sometimes the simplest form of justice was to let people expose their own ignorance.

He signed into the Ap Exchange. Thirty-two new apps had been uploaded. As usual, a fair amount were vision powers, mostly duplicates of stuff he already had. It turned out to be relatively easy to tweak a retina to see in infrared or ultraviolet. But what he really needed now was something no one had yet effectively cobbled together.

He opened a chat box and typed, "X-ray vision. See through thirty feet of steel. Possible?" He hit send.

Instantly, people on the forum started responding.

Sidekick: "Nope."

BruceBanner: "What you need are gamma rays."

Code4U: "Steel>gamma ray penetration."

TheYellowKid: "Seismic imaging might work."

BruceBanner: "Neutrinos?"

Sidekick: "How 2 capture?"

TheYellowKid: "4 iron, something like magnavision?"

Sidekick: "Like!"

BruceBanner: "I'll upload by midnight."

Code4U: That long? I'm already banging out code.

BruceBanner: "It's on."

Found a pistol in the rubble. A .22
revolver, intact. Most gun parts I find
are mangled where I bit through them.
Three bullets, but I bet I can find more
out here if I look for them.
Out here? In here?
The gun will come in handy in catching
those damn chickens. I might could have
caught them on earth, but out here (in
here?) they can actually get some
distance with those wings. I've already
lost all the darts I was throwing at
them.
Funny thing is, I've had a lot of guns
in my hand, but I don't think I've ever
shot anyone or anything. But how hard can
it be?

Chapter Six
The Kind of Dance Where You Take Your Clothes Off

THEY WERE AT A REST AREA in southern Ohio when the cop spotted them. The rest area wasn't much, just a couple of cinderblock outhouses with no running water. There were some cement picnic tables under an oak tree, all cracked up, crumbling, and covered with bird poop. They had their Harley parked next to the tables, well away from the official parking spaces. Thanksgiving was only a week away, and they were near the mountains, so Pit had expected the weather to be chilly. Instead, the day had passed from pleasantly warm into flat-out hot at some point. When the weather was cold, it was no big deal. Sunday could keep them warm. When it was hot, alas, her thermostat only ran in one direction.

It was mid afternoon and Sunday had stretched out on the table top with her jacked under her head to catch a nap. They'd been racing down highways more or less at random, picking new roads purely on the impulses of his fractured brain. They hadn't exactly been discreet as Pit had adopted a standard cruising speed just shy of 110 mph. That was the speed the Harley wanted to go, a speed where he felt like the bike was flying. They'd put over 8,000 miles on the bike in two weeks. It was nearly impossible that no cop had seen them. Why hadn't they been ambushed yet? The suspense was killing him.

Then a Highway Patrol car pulled into the rest area. The cop parked, got out of his cruiser, glanced in their direction, then froze. The cop very, very, very slowly lowered himself back into his driver's seat, fastened his seat belt, then drove out of the rest stop at a moderate rate of speed, his head never turning in their direction.

Pit thought this was peculiar. Had the cop seen them or hadn't he? Then Pit figured it out. The cop had seen them. Probably so had a hundred others. Each of them had to know, by this point, that Pit and Sunday had a reputation for leaving behind a trail of widows. It was also well established that Devourer and Burn Baby never struck twice in the same town. For most cops, it was probably an easy choice to act like they hadn't seen anything.

After Sunday woke, they headed south, across the Ohio river into West Virginia., After nightfall, Pit wound up pretty much as lost as a person could get, after taking a wrong turn off Highway 23 and winding up on a road so full of switchbacks that Pit really had no idea where they were headed. The gas was getting low. And, of course, Sunday was complaining about how hungry and tired she was. Pit had no problem with just pulling off the road and sleeping under a tree and his dietary needs weren't particularly dainty. Sunday, on the other hand, refused to eat roadkill, which Pit thought was a bit snooty of her, especially since she of all people wouldn't have to eat it raw. Sunday was also insistent that they sleep in a place with a real bed and an actual bathroom. She'd been nagging Pit to take a shower every day, which was just crazy, and who was she, his mother? But he went along with her agenda without a grumble. As long as they were robbing a bank every couple of days, he was having fun.

But was it just for robbing banks that they were still together? From what memories Pit could assemble, they'd always parted ways quickly in the past following their annual meet-ups. Sunday had been focused on Monday's mission, and she'd had little patience for Pit's meandering approach to life.

Now, if Monday really had dismissed them from duty, Sunday was just as lost and directionless as he was. He wasn't a guy known for his deep insights into the minds of women, but he couldn't help but think that Sunday was with him still because she didn't know where else to be. In all his aimless wandering, he secretly hoped he might one day turn down a road and find himself in front of a familiar house. He would suddenly realize, "This is the house I grew up in." Or, "This is the house I lived in when I got married." Somewhere on one of these roads, he would find the key. The gates of his mind would swing open, and he'd know his past.

And Sunday?

Somewhere, on one of these roads, she was hoping to find the sign that pointed toward her future.

For now, on this particular road, he would have been happy to find a sign that pointed toward any recognizable destination at all. He'd been lost in the boondocks before, but this was getting ridiculous.

Just as he was on the verge of stopping the bike and admitting that he didn't know where the hell he was so that Sunday could fly up and look around for nearby towns, he spotted lights through the branches of the trees on a ridge above them. He gunned the bike up the curves, arriving at a structure that looked like an old gas station that someone had nailed a bunch of planks to. A wooden sign in front declared it to be the Hillbilly Hideout. In smaller letters it read "B-B-Q and Beer." A half-dozen pick-up trucks were parked in the gravel lot.

"Dinner time," he said, as he pulled the bike in beside a beat up Ford.

"I was hoping we could find a hotel first," said Sunday. She looked exhausted, and she'd been quiet all day.

"I'll ask how to get to the nearest one," he said.

"Damn," she said, getting off the bike. "You asking for directions? This I gotta see."

As they approached the door, he heard loud country music thumping from inside.

"Oh lord," Sunday moaned. "I'm not sure I'm up for this."

"What's wrong?"

She crossed her arms. "Nothing. I'm just tired. Tired of greasy road food. Tired of being on that bike twelve hours a day. This road we've been on tonight must surely be the intestines of America. I say the next big town we reach, we steal a plane and head for France."

"You speak French?"

She shook her head. "But French cops probably scare even easier than American cops. When we aren't working, the food's got to be better."

"It's all the same to me," said Pit. "I really can't taste anything."

"Your taste buds have probably been killed off by all the crap you put in your mouth."

"Maybe," said Pit. "The thing is, the food doesn't really go in my mouth. Every now and then, I feel a tickle at the back of my throat, especially when I'm pulling stuff out, but I really don't think the stuff I eat goes in my stomach at all."

"Then where does it go?"

Pit shrugged.

"I mean, some of it must go in you. You haven't starved."

"Maybe. But what's weird is that I haven't used the bathroom since I woke up on the side of a highway back in 1956."

She stared at him.

"Honest," he said. "I don't even pee."

"Okay," she said. "That's either way more information than I needed, or the most fascinating thing I've ever learned about you. Seriously? Never?"

"Nope."

"Wow," she said, eying the door. "Let's go in. Suddenly I need a beer."

"I thought you didn't drink."

"Ordinarily I don't," she said. "But with any luck I'm going to kill the brain cells that have latched onto the mystery of your excretory functions."

They opened the door to the strains of "Achy Breaky Heart." Sunday sighed.

The place was a dive, even by Pit's standards. There were about three light bulbs total working in the place. What he'd assumed to be a jukebox was an iPod plugged into a boombox sitting on a bar stool. There were eight or nine guys in the room, all middle-aged rednecks with beer guts. Some were sitting at a bar, but most were clustered around a pool table, though not to shoot pool. Instead, there was a teenage girl dancing drunkenly in the center of the table stripped down to her bra and panties, which were stuffed with dollar bills. She was a little on the chunky side, her belly covered with stretch marks, a square-faced blonde wearing too much make up. She looked the way Tammy Faye Bakker must have looked when she was sixteen.

Half of the men in the room turned their heads to see who'd just come through the door, and the other half continued to ogle the dancing girl.

Pit turned around and placed his hand on Sunday's shoulder. "Let's find another place."

"We're here," she said firmly, pushing past him and heading toward the bar.

The girl on the table stopped dancing. The men all stared at Sunday.

"Got any Red Stripe?" Sunday asked the man behind the counter, a squat bald man with an eye patch. The sleeves of his red long johns hung out of his filthy white V-neck tee shirt.

"Red Stripe? You mean the gum?" Eye-patch asked.

"There's a gum named Red Stripe?" Sunday asked. She was shouting to be heard over the music, but the song ended and she was simply shouting.

"We don't got no gum," said Eye-patch.

"Red Stripe's a beer," Sunday said. For some reason, the music hadn't started back up again.

"We got Bud and PBR."

Sunday pursed her lips, pondering her options.

"PBR," she said. "And a barbeque sandwich."

"We ain't got no barbeque."

"Your sign—"

"Kitchen's closed." He crossed his arms. "We serve breakfast and lunch. At night, we turn the joint over to private parties."

One of the men at the pool table staggered over. He had a half-empty Mason jar in his hand, full of clear liquid that made Pit's eyes water.

"I'm Root," he said, his speech slurred. "It's my birthday.

You're welcome to stay."

"How old's that girl?" Sunday asked.

"I don't rightly know," said Root. He belched. "It ain't polite to ask a woman her age."

"How old are you, girl?" Sunday asked.

"Old enough," the girl said, crossing her arms.

"If we had an older woman," Root said, looking Sunday up and down, "she'd be more than welcome to dance."

Pit put his hand on Sunday's arm. "If y'all ain't got no food, we'll just be moving on," he announced.

By now, two of the beefier men had moved to stand in front of the door.

"What's your hurry?" asked Root. "You just got here. This party's just getting started."

"We're just looking for dinner," said Pit. "Didn't really come to dance."

"All women like dancing," said Root.

"She doesn't," said Pit.

"You talk for her?" Root asked.

"He doesn't talk for me," said Sunday.

"Then, what do you say? You want to dance?"

By now, Eye-patch had produced the can of PBR. Sunday took it, popped the top, and downed it while she contemplated Root's question.

"This would be a dance where I take off my clothes?" she asked, wiping her mouth.

"Well, sure, if you wanted to. Sure. The kind of dance where you take off your clothes would be just fine."

Pit tried to pull Sunday toward the door, but she twisted her arm free.

At the door, one of the large men pushed aside his jacket and revealed a pistol.

"Why don't you have a seat, Mister?" the gunman said.

"I reckon I will," said Pit. He raised himself onto a stool, suddenly looking forward to what was about to happen. In his opinion, once a man pulled out a gun, he deserved whatever was coming his way.

Sunday had taken off her jacket and laid it on the bar. She was wearing a tight black sweater beneath this that showed off her curves. She took a seat on a stool and began to unzip her boots. Someone started the music back up. "Six Days on the Road" by Dave Dudley. It had been years since Pit had heard this song.

The girl on the table placed her hands on her hips. "Root, I ain't splitting the money."

"I dance for free," said Sunday, standing up barefoot on a floor that even Pit Geek thought looked germy.

She unbuttoned her jeans and peeled them off. This was normally the time in a bank robbery where she would start glowing. She wasn't using her powers yet. Pit noticed that her new leg had darkened up a little, but was still a lot whiter than her other leg.

"She's not even dancing!" the girl complained. "She's just taking off her clothes!"

Sunday pulled off her sweater. The girl on the table started grinding her butt up against an imaginary pole, trying to regain the room's attention, but no one was looking at her now.

Sunday reached up and cupped her bra, pressing her breasts together. If Pit had been a fair judge, he would have to admit that the girl on the table had nicer jugs. Still, Sunday won the rest of the body competition hands down.

Root was practically drooling. "Oh mama," he said. "Baby, you should be a model."

Sunday glanced back at Pit. "For the record, that's much more flattering than you telling me I could be a prostitute."

"Aw, what do I know about talking to women?" Pit said.

Sunday removed her bra. Sweat beaded on Root's forehead. The song shifted to "You Never Even Called Me By My Name."

"You like what you see?" Sunday asked.

"What a damn awesome birthday," Root mumbled.

"Want to touch?"

Root reached with thick, trembling fingers toward her dark areola.

Then Pit couldn't see anything. Root was screaming. The girl on the table started shrieking. The boom box squealed as its electronics were fried by the ions flooding the room. There was a gunshot to Pit's left. Then another, and another, then a scream cut short. The room took on the smell of burnt bacon.

Pit rubbed his eyes, trying to get rid of the dancing spots. "Christ almighty," he grumbled. "You'd think I'd of learned by now to keep my eyes closed."

Sunday laughed, her voice only a few feet away. "My father told me you were a slow learner."

When Sunday vaporized a human being completely, it was a curiously soft sound, almost like a feather pillow being tossed onto a bed, a gentle "*fumph.*"

Fumph. Fumph. Fumph. Fumph. And maybe a few he'd missed over the girl's shrieking.

He finally got his eyes working. The room was a lot emptier. The cinder block walls were painted with sooty human shadows, men running, mostly.

Root was still alive, on his knees, both hands missing. His eyes had burst, leaving a trail of red and white goop streaming down his cheeks. He was drawing deep breaths and looked like he was screaming, but only gurgles came out.

The girl was still alive. She'd dropped to her hands and knees. Sunday let the plasma surrounding her flicker out. Pit tried not to stare at Sunday's naked crotch, but found he really couldn't help it.

Sunday grabbed the girl by the hair. "Give me the money," she said.

"What?" the girl sobbed.

"The money in your underwear! Give it to me!"

"Oh god don't kill me," the girl whimpered.

"Give me the money!" Sunday screamed.

The girl's hands were shaking so badly she dropped half the bills as she pulled them from her panties. Sunday scooped them into a little pile and counted them, slapping the bills on the worn green felt of the table. Pit could see they were mostly ones.

"Thirty-seven dollars," Sunday said, shaking her head. "You'd sell your body for thirty-seven dollars?"

"No!" the girl protested. "They were just watching! They couldn't . . . you know, touch me for a couple of dollar bills."

"Then for what?" Sunday asked.

The girl sniffled. "I don't know. Maybe a hundred? Maybe fifty?"

Sunday bunched the bills into her fist which suddenly flared, singing the girl's hair. The girl tried to crawl away, but Sunday grabbed her by the face, smearing the dark mascara tracks that ran down her cheeks in an eerie echo of Root's fate.

"I don't know!" the girl cried. "I don't know how much to charge!"

"I'm not quizzing you on the proper fees!" Sunday screamed. Spittle flew from her lips. "No price! No price! No one should be commodity to be bought or sold! I've been fighting since I was no older than you trying to break the world free from its thinly disguised economy of slavery and here you are! Here you are, selling yourself! Why? Why?"

"I've got a little girl at home," the dancer sobbed. "I need money for her."

Sunday slowly released the girl's face.

"Was one of these men the father?" she asked.

"No," the girl said, wiping her snot from her face. "He's my age."

Sunday stared at the black mascara smudges on her fingers. She wiped them on the pool table.

She walked toward Pit. He made a show of hiding his eyes behind his hand as he held her jeans toward her.

"Oh, go ahead and look," she grumbled. "You think I didn't see you staring?"

"Sorry," said Pit.

"You're not sorry." She pulled on her jeans in one fluid motion.

"Naw, I'm not."

She pulled on her sweater without bothering with her bra. She sat on the stool to put her boots on. "I hate all mankind."

"There's always Monkeyland," said Pit.

She gave him a sideways glance, started to say something, then stopped.

Pit looked at Root. He was still breathing, still sitting up, and maybe, against all odds, still conscious."

"You going to put him out of his misery?"

"Not planning on it," she said.

"What about the girl?"

"I don't give a damn what she does," said Sunday, with a dismissive wave.

On hearing this, the girl rolled off the table and crawled toward the door. Sunday zipped up her boots as the girl slipped outside.

"There might be some food in the kitchen," Pit said, going behind the bar. The kitchen was little more than a sink, a microwave, and a small refrigerator. In the fridge, he found a pack of hot dogs. He also found a door to the gravel lot out back, standing open.

"You want a wiener?" he called out to her.

"Since you aren't smart enough for innuendo, I assume you've found hot dogs?"

"Yeah."

"I'm really not hungry now," she said. "We never did ask where we could find a hotel."

"Hey," said Pit, staring at the open door. "Did you kill the guy with the eye-patch?"

"Uhhhh, no. I don't think so. I think he bolted while I was focused on the guy with the gun."

Pit Geek sighed. "I bet he's called the cops by now."

"Why should we care?" asked Sunday. "Let them come."

She shook her head as she stared at the pool table. "Let them send the whole damn army." She looked down at her hands and let twin balls of glowing plasma bubble up in her palms. "I think . . . I think I've crossed a line, Pit."

"How so?" he said, coming back from the kitchen.

"I thought this was war," she said, so softly he could barely hear her. "I thought I was saving the innocent and ignorant masses from the machinations of secretive, powerful men who treated them like animals." She sighed. "But they were animals all along. Mad, bad, dangerous animals who need to be put down."

"Monday really screwed you up," said Pit.

"Monday gave me purpose. Monday gave me hope."

Pit shook his head. "Monday made you think that things were important. But nothing's really important. These folks tonight were just passing time as best they could until the Grim Reaper came for 'em. No one gets out of this world alive, so what's it matter how you spend your days? Just do what you like to do. If these guys liked looking at some girl shaking her ass, and she liked shaking it, why not let them have their fun?"

Sunday rolled the plasma around in her palm as she thought his words over. "That some kind of cowboy philosophy?"

"I dunno where I heard it," said Pit. "Maybe it's in the Bible?"

"I'm fairly certain it's not," Sunday said, chuckling. "Let's get out of here. I've never been so tired in all my life."

They stepped out of the bar and walked toward the Harley. When they were ten feet away, a large man in white tights dropped down from the sky and landed on the bike, flattening it. A cloud of dust rose from the impact. Pit and Sunday stopped dead in their tracks.

The man in white rose from his crouching position in the shallow crater as dust and shreds of pulverized Harley drifted down around him. He was tall and bulging with muscles, with a square jaw and close-cropped ink-black hair that made him look like he'd stepped out of a comic book. There was a large red S in the center of his chest.

"Pit Geek," the man said, in a deep bass voice. "Sundancer. You're under arrest. I'd advise you to surrender. Lethal force has been authorized for your capture."

"You've got us confused with somebody else," Pit said. "We're Devourer and Burn Baby."

"Baby Burn," said Sunday. Then she looked at the big guy. "You found us. Can you catch us?"

The man in white blurred. Before either of them could blink, he'd grabbed Sunday by the wrist.

"Not bad," said Sunday. "But can you hold us?"

Pit remembered to close his eyes this time, but even still the flash felt like lightning burning into the back of his skull. He shielded his eyes with his hands as he carefully opened them. Sunday was nothing but a glowing outline. The ground beneath her bubbled like a pool of lava.

The man in white still had hold of her wrist. Not a single hair on his head was singed.

Pit couldn't be sure, but it looked like Sunday smiled at her captor.

"You're going to be a lot more fun than an army," she said.

I found seventeen bullets. Nine left.
Shooting a moving chicken ain't as easy
as you'd think.

Chapter Seven
Hounded by Heroes

PIT HAD TAKEN a few steps back when Sunday burst into flames. Now he jumped forward, mouth wide open, intending to bite the big man's arm off. However, before he'd closed the gap between them even an inch, he was kicked in the nose by a blue leather boot with thick rubber soles. The boot had come from above and as he hit the ground on his back he found himself gazing up at a woman in a sky-blue flight suit and dark-blue helmet, with her face hidden by a mirrored visor that showed the blood gushing from his nose. There was something dark behind him, and he turned his head to see he'd just missed bouncing his skull off the front tire of a Chevy El Dorado.

Before he could rise, a short black kid in red tights came out of nowhere and jumped on his left arm, pressing Pit's hand to the ground. The kid shouted, "Glue mode!" Instantly the kid's hands turned gooey, like his flesh had changed to paste as he ran his fingers all over Pit's knuckles. Pit's free hand reached for the kid's neck and grabbed hold, and began dragging the young hero's throat toward his mouth. The kid pressed Pit's gunked up hand against the truck tire and shouted, "Ghost mode!" Pit's hand suddenly slipped right through the kid and he wound up slapping himself in his already broken nose.

The guy in red bounced to his feet. Pit tried to rise, but found his hand thoroughly stuck to the tire.

"Shame we messed up your plastic surgery," the kid said. "As a fellow film buff, I appreciated the tribute."

"What the hell are you talking about?" Pit asked, still trying to yank his hand free.

"Hello?" said the kid. "Frank Macey? The Stick-Em-Up Kid?"

The woman in blue swooped down. "We're here to arrest them, Ap, not talk film trivia. Switch to foam mode. Servant's got his hands full."

"Foam mode," said Ap as the woman dropped behind him and wrapped her arms around his torso. "Sorry, Skyrider."

They shot into the air a hundred feet, which happened to be where Sundancer had flown, with Servant in tow. Pit shielded his eyes with his free hand as he stared up. Sunday was spinning in violent gyrations; she'd never been able to keep her balance with someone else in tow. However, her dizzying spirals turned out to be an effective strategy. Servant suddenly went flying off, leaving a trail of vomit.

Sundancer stabilized her flight, shaking her fist at him as he crashed into the forest below and started bouncing down the steep mountain slope. "I hope you break your damn neck!" she cried.

But, with her attention focused on Servant, she failed to notice that Skyrider and Ap were now hovering directly above her. Ap was completely coated head to toe in what looked like shaving cream. He opened his mouth and buckets of the white foam shot out of him, catching Sunday in the torrent.

"Son of a bitch," Sunday cursed as she began to tumble wildly through the sky. The foam boiled off seconds after it hit her, but the unevenness of the heat she was producing was messing with her ability to stay airborne. Skyrider did an impressive job of following the flaming woman's dizzying path through the air, and more and more foam found its target on Sunday's face. Sunday coughed and gasped and spit as she wiped her eyes, trying to rid herself of the goop.

"Keep foaming her!" Skyrider shouted. "She needs to breathe like anyone else!"

Pit was distracted by a loud whoosh to his right. He turned and saw a white blur flash up the road and enter the parking lot, skidding to a halt at the rear wheel of the truck Pit was glued to.

"This guy's going to need new tires anyway," Servant said as he put his right hand under the rear bumper and lifted the back of the truck. Servant ripped the wheel right off the hub, sending lug nuts shooting across the gravel lot.

"Naw, he won't," said Pit, thinking about the black shadows on the wall of the bar.

Servant wasted no time on further banter. He drew the tire back like it was a discus and let it rip. The tire caught Sunday right in the gut and she went flying, missing Skyrider and Ap by a whisker. Her body was limp, folded across the tire, as she cut a long glowing arc through the sky, her flames sputtering and dimming. They went dark completely as she crashed into the forest.

"Servant!" Skyrider shouted. "You nearly hit us!"

"But I didn't," he said.

"We almost had her!" she shouted back.

"I definitely got her," said Servant.

Ap spit out a few last cupfuls of foam, then wiped his mouth. "That tire couldn't even have touched her if I hadn't cooled her off!"

Servant shrugged and crossed his arms. "So it was teamwork."

"Let's just find her," said Ap. "Infra-eye mode!" He looked in the direction she'd flown.

Pit Geek looked toward the bar. He said to Servant, "You got some way of calling an ambulance?"

"You'll get all the medical attention you require," said Servant, watching Skyrider and Ap disappear into the trees.

"I was thinking about that poor guy in the bar."

Servant cocked his head toward the door. Smoke was still drifting from the building. Servant picked up a piece of what had once been the Harley's frame and started bending it. He crouched in front of Pit and twisted the metal around his face, covering from just below his eyes to just above his throat, crimping the metal behind Pit's neck. Pit noticed that Servant didn't have a single scorch mark or even any dirt on his costume after bouncing down the mountain.

Servant stood up, looking at Pit's immobilized hand, and probably thought he was being clever when he said, "Don't go anywhere."

Servant went into the bar. His white tights glowed in the darkened doorway. Servant stopped moving. For some reason, his tights turned dark.

"Dear God," he whispered.

He came out of the bar a moment later cradling Root in his arms. For reasons that Pit couldn't even guess at, Servant was buck naked. His muscular body was covered in thick black kinky hair over pale green flesh. His uncircumcised genitals were monstrously large. Worse, his face had lost its square-jawed comic book handsomeness and been replaced by a misshapen skull covered with leathery green skin. He revealed a mouthful of jagged fangs as he snarled at Pit, "What kind of monsters are you?"

"The bad kind, I reckon," said Pit, his voice muffled by his metal gag.

Servant pressed his lips tightly together. He took a deep breath through the gaping hole in his face where his nose should have been. Then, the air around him rippled and he was back in costume, his face once more human. Servant turned into a blur as he darted down the road, leaving a cloud of dust in the parking lot. Pit had no idea how far they were from the nearest hospital or even which direction to head, but apparently Servant knew.

Pit twisted his neck, pushing the metal gag tighter against his lips. Servant had apparently been under the misconception that Pit had to get something between his teeth to bite it. Instead, he puckered his lips and sucked. The metal gag spiraled down his mouth like it was vanishing down a toilet.

He was about to start nibbling at the rubber around his hand to free himself when Skyrider burst back above the tree line. She was carrying something in her arms, but it was too dark to make out what. A few seconds later, a large round shape like a balloon twenty feet across drifted into the air behind her.

Skyrider zoomed back to the parking lot, landing in the gravel in front of Pit with a soft crunch. She carried Sunday in her arms. Sunday was completely limp, her face and body flecked with baked on foam that looked like dark brown meringue. She was covered with a hundred scratch marks from where she'd fallen through the trees. Her face was spattered with red goop, as if she'd been lying on her back drinking a bottle of ketchup, then coughed it out. Her open eyes stared blankly toward the stars. The skin of her face was now the same pale shade as her restored leg.

Skyrider placed Sundancer in the bed of the pick up truck. There was a blue plastic tarp wadded up in one corner of the bed. She unfolded this, covering the body.

"She's dead," said Pit.

"Neither of you could really have expected you'd be getting out of this alive," said Skyrider, her voice strangely hollow, almost mechanical.

"No one gets out alive," said Pit, looking up at the dark sky.

He spotted Ap bouncing along the tree tops. The top of the boy's head had swollen up into a balloon. It apparently left him buoyant enough to run along the very tips of the branches. Ap jumped out over the parking lot and drifted down behind the pickup that held Sunday's corpse. "End Airhead Mode," he said. With a sound like a whoopee cushion, his head deflated back to its normal dimensions in barely a second.

"Where's Servant?" he asked.

"The big guy remembered an appointment elsewhere," said Pit.

Ap looked ill. "Did you . . . did you eat him?"

"Naw," Pit chuckled. "He ran some guy we half killed off to a hospital."

Skyrider sighed. "Damn it. He could be anywhere."

"Just call him," said Ap.

"He doesn't carry a phone!"

"Right. What's up with that?"

Skyrider shook her head. "He doesn't have any pockets."

"Hello," said Ap. "That can't be that hard to fix. Our engineers can repair teleportation belts. Certainly they can master the technology of the pocket."

"Servant doesn't wear pants," said Skyrider.

"He just needs a utility belt," said Ap.

"Anything that doesn't slide off his force fields gets chewed up by his time flux. A belt wouldn't last half an hour on him."

"He could just tuck it into his tights," said Ap, sounding exasperated that Skyrider was making such lame excuses for why a teammate couldn't carry a phone.

She looked toward Pit, as if making sure he was still secure, then back to Ap. "I guess it won't hurt for you to know. Servant doesn't wear tights. All clothes just fall off of him. Luckily, he can make his force fields opaque and change their colors."

Ap grinned. "You mean Mr. Holier-Than-Thou prances around in public completely naked?"

She nodded. "And if something breaks his concentration, his fields go transparent!" She laughed. "Oh god. You can't know how much I was sweating through that press conference, praying that he wouldn't get a question that rattled him."

Ap burst into laughter, snorting as he wiped tears from his eyes. "Shit," he sighed. "Is there something seriously wrong with me that I find this mildly arousing?"

Skyrider shook her head. "I've gotten a good look at his junk. The porn industry suffered a tragic loss the day that man picked up a Bible."

Pit found it highly disrespectful that they were laughing so hard while Sunday's body lay in front of them. On the other hand, they'd both completely forgotten about him. Biting the tire would pop it, and catch their attention.

So he bit his left hand off at the wrist. As usual, there was a half-hearted trickle of blood, then the wound dried up. He jammed his right hand into his mouth and felt around the pile of junk. He'd always been able to pull out the stuff he'd eaten, though he sometimes spent an hour or more pulling out crap before he found what he wanted. Luckily, one of the last things he'd swallowed in that vault in Columbus had been a gold brick. The thing weighed about thirty pounds but was still small enough to wrap his fist around it. He lunged to his feet as he pulled his hand from his mouth.

Skyrider had her back to him. Ap's eyes went wide. The kid

opened his mouth to scream a warning but Pit was already in full swing. She spun and Pit drove the gold bar just below the edge of her helmet into her throat. The Kevlar collar gave some padding, but it felt to Pit like he flattened her trachea against her vertebrae. She dropped to the gravel on one knee, clutching her throat.

Pit vaulted onto the bed of the pickup, then lunged for Ap.

"Ghost mode," the kid yelped.

Pit flew right through the boy, scratching his face up as he crashed into the gravel.

"Stonefist mode!" The kid screamed, as Pit rose to his knees. He fell back down as Ap punched him just above the ear. He rolled in the gravel, cursing, "Shit! Shit! Shit!" It felt like he'd been hit with a sledgehammer.

"Spike-toe mode!" the boy shouted. The tips of his black boots tore apart as sharp shafts that reminded Pit of little rhino horns tore through the leather.

The boy drew his leg back. With a loud grunt, he kicked Pit in the nuts, the spike toes digging in all the way to Pit's left kidney.

"Sweet merciful Jesus," Pit wheezed as he fell, curling into a fetal ball.

"Web mode!" Ap shouted. The stars in front of Pit's eyes were just starting to clear when the boy began to spit on him, in long sticky strips that draped across Pit and clung to the gravel around him.

Luckily for Pit, the kid couldn't spit all that far, and gravel is a piss-poor base to try to stick someone to. Pit rose up on his left elbow, lifting up the gravel without effort, and whipped his right arm out to grab Ap by the ankle.

"Ghost—" Ap screamed, but it was too late. Pit jerked his leg toward his mouth and took it off at the ankle.

Ap shrieked in utter terror as he fell, blood spurting from his severed limb.

"Stop being such a crybaby," Pit grumbled as he dragged himself forward, then shoved another six inches of the kid's leg into his mouth. This time, he'd just keep sucking until he reached the kid's lungs. After getting punched in the head, the last thing Pit needed was this piercing high-pitched screaming.

"Ghost mode!" Ap cried. "Ghost mode!"

Pit's fingers lost their grip on the boy's leg. The boy was still sitting before him, his eyes staring in horror at his mangled limb, but Pit's hands passed right through him. Pit groaned as he sat up.

The boy was sobbing, but for some reason he had stopped bleeding. Maybe he just didn't have blood in ghost mode.

"Aw, don't take it so hard," said Pit, holding up the stump of his left forearm. "I've lost lots of limbs. You ain't gonna die." Then, he remembered that it wasn't to his advantage to comfort the kid. "I mean, you are gonna die, if you turn solid again. Next time, I'll bite off your head."

"Exit," the boy sobbed. "Exit!"

And then he wasn't there. Pit furrowed his brow. He knew this command. The kid had just been snatched back to safety by Rex Monday's space machine. What the hell? Were these three super-powered goons working for his old boss?

He limped around the truck, his legs wobbly as Jell-O. He'd been kicked in the nuts lots of times, but, Christ, this kid had practically neutered him. Skyrider was gone, probably snatched away by the space machine. Servant might be back any second. Pit didn't really have time to wait until he was feeling better. He reached his right hand back into his mouth and felt around until his fingers closed around the handle of a gun. He pulled it back out, carrying the regeneration ray. He tossed aside the blue tarp. Sunday's limp and lifeless form made his throat tighten. Her torso was all jumbled up, as if every rib had been broken. He leaned against the side of the truck to keep his arm steady as he aimed at her. He pressed his lips together and tried to ignore his various pains as the lights danced across Sunday's body. The time dragged by with tortuous slowness as the machine announced each stage of her reconstruction.

At last, the gun was done. He stuffed the ray back into his mouth. Sunday's body was restored. It looked like she was merely sleeping, but there was no movement at all in her chest.

Was she breathing? Pit crawled into the truck bed, lying on her as he pressed his fingers to her throat. No pulse.

"Wake up," he cried, crouching over her. He raised his fist and drove it into her ribs right under her left breast. He knelt down, placing the stump of his arm under her neck to tilt her head up. He took a deep breath and placed his mouth on hers. Fortunately, he had to actively try to devour things, otherwise his mouth was just a mouth. He sealed his lips to hers and pinched her nose shut, blowing air into her lungs. He did this three times, then straddled her, preparing to push on her chest.

She turned her head.

"Sunny?" he asked.

Her eyelashes fluttered open. She looked around, her eyes glazed. She finally focused on him. She sat up. Their faces were inches apart.

"You're alive!" he cried, and fell upon her, grabbing her by the back of her neck and planting a huge kiss on her mouth. Then, his body tensed up, as he anticipated vaporization.

He drew his face back from hers.

Her eyes were wide, frightened.

"Was I dead?" she whispered.

"Looked like it."

She nodded, took a deep breath, and slowly the fear drained from her face. She looked at his broken nose. "Well, your new look didn't last long."

"We'll use the ray on it later," Pit said, lifting himself off of her. "Servant could be back any second."

"Right," she said, as she took his extended hand to help her rise. "Where's the Harley?"

"Flattened, remember?" Pit said as he limped to the door of the truck. "You know how to hotwire a vehicle?"

"No," she said, as she scooted toward the edge of the bed.

Pit laughed at he looked at the steering column. The keys were in the ignition!

"This must be a safe neighborhood," he said. "Get in."

Sunday supported herself on the edge of the truck as she walked gingerly across the cold gravel to the passenger door.

She got into the truck and looked down at Pit's crotch as she fastened her seatbelt.

"Oh god," she said, her face turning green as the dashboard lights came on. "What happened?"

"You shoulda seen the other guy," Pit said. He threw the truck into gear and lurched backward onto the road, then put the truck into drive and stomped the gas. The truck tires squealed to hold onto the asphalt as they raced down the curvy road. Sunday grabbed the dashboard. "I'd rather not die in a car crash!"

"We can't be near here when Servant comes back," Pit said as he jerked the truck around another curve.

His words proved prophetic. At that exact instant a white blur flashed into their headlights. On pure instinct, Pit gunned the motor. Half a second later they each had a face full of air bags as Servant slammed into the grill, shattered the windshield, then bounced over the roof. The big man slammed into the truck bed, grabbed the blue tarp, then slipped out into thin air. Apparently, his force fields really were kind of slick. Pit continued racing forward blindly until he sucked down the airbag that obstructed his view. The truck was still running, but white steam was pouring from under the hood. The check engine light came on, as well as a little red thermometer next to it.

"Keep driving," said Sunday, unbuckling her seat belt. "Try to get at least a mile away. Two or three if the truck can make it."

"What are you. . . ?" he never got to finish his question. She pushed her door open and jumped out.

Pit remembered to shut his eyes. When he opened them, it was as bright as midday. The truck seemed to be losing power. Pressing the petal to the floor only produced a top speed of sixty, then fifty, then forty. He kept driving without glancing into his rear view as flaming magma began to rain down around him. Trees each side of him suddenly exploded into flame. The temperature in the truck cab grew unbearable. He reached for the AC button. The second he pressed it, the engine seized up. He threw the truck into neutral and rolled another half mile down the mountain before he reached a slight uphill grade and drifted to a stop. He got out and looked back at he mountain he'd just come down. Was it just his imagination that the mountain now looked significantly shorter? It was hard to tell with all the smoke. Every tree in the area was on fire.

Light flickered behind the dark haze. Sunday suddenly dropped from the smoke. Her hands and forearms went dark and she grabbed Pit beneath his armpits. They shot up into the sky.

"You can't fly and carry me!" he shouted.

"If Skyrider can fucking carry passengers, I can fucking carry passengers," she growled. They punched through the roiling smoke into a clear night. Pit noticed their path through the sky was still weaving back and forth, but it was certainly nothing like the vomit inducing spin she'd put Servant through earlier.

He shouted above the wind, "What happened to the big guy?"

She was panting as she said, "I kept my distance. Since he couldn't fly, I tried melting the asphalt to trap his feet but he kept jumping free. He threw a couple of big rocks at me, but I melted them. So, I decided to melt the mountain top and drown him in hot lava. He swam to the surface a couple of times, but I think I got him."

"Did he ever turn naked?" Pit asked.

"That . . . is the oddest thing . . . I've ever . . . been asked," she said. She was really straining to breathe now. They were dropping lower and lower over the tree line.

"You doing okay?"

"Not really," she said, as they inched even closer to the ground. "I got kind of dizzy . . . when I cooled off to pick you up. That a lake . . . up ahead?"

Pit Geek strained to see through the flickering radiance surrounding them. He did see a dark patch on the ground ahead that might be water.

"Hold onto . . . your ass," she mumbled. "In case of . . . a water landing . . . your seat . . . flotation—"

They hit the water at a shallow angle, bouncing along it like a stone before they sank. Pit pushed his head back above the surface and gasped. Sunday bobbed up next to him barely ten feet away, face down. He swam toward her and turned her limp body over, so that she now faced the sky. She coughed. "I can't believe . . . that worked," she whispered.

As Pit kicked his feet around, he realized that his toes kept hitting bottom. He stopped flailing and stood up. The water only came to his nipples. It was ice cold, which numbed the pain in his groin. He cradled Sunday in his arms and said, "Shore's this way."

He carried her onto a bank covered with pine needles. Behind them was a row of log cabins. No lights were on anywhere.

"This kind of looks like a boy scout camp," he said. "Looks empty."

She pushed against his chest, indicating she wanted to be put down. Her legs were rubbery as she started stumbling toward the nearest cabin. "Empty or not, we're sleeping here. I'm not feeling so hot."

Pit glanced back toward the glow on the horizon. The mountain she'd set on fire had to be at least fifty miles away. They'd really been moving.

Sunday melted the lock off the cabin door. Inside looked like a meeting room, with the whole back wall being one enormous stone fireplace. A green cloth banner above the mantle read, "Christ is King."

Sunday dropped to her knees on the big rug in front of the fireplace, then collapsed face down. Pit climbed up onto the fireplace and tore down the banner. He draped it over her like a blanket.

He saw a chalkboard next to the door they'd come in. He walked to it and saw a stick of white chalk in the tray.

"What are you doing?" Sunday whispered.

"Don't trust my memory," he said. "Wanna write something down."

In rough block letters he wrote, "FRANK MACY. STICK-M-UP KID."

He moved to the window. "I'll keep watch," he said.

"If they find us, they find us," she murmured. "Get some

sleep."

Pit moved back to the rug and sat down.

"Lie down," she said.

He lay down.

She pressed herself against him, laying her head on his good arm, draping an arm and a leg across his body.

"I can't sleep without a pillow," she said, her voice soft and distant.

Five seconds later, she began to snore.

Found a black boot today with a foot
inside of it. It has to belong to Ap. I
found it next to a wallet that has a
license in it that expired in 1972.
Andrew Kermit Bergman. Lived in Tampa.
Was I in Florida during that time?
All the strata have been jumbled up. So
much for the hope I could crawl from one
edge of my memories to the other and find
a coherent path.
Things I do remember eating:
The hood ornament off a Jaguar.
A diamond ring with the woman's finger
still inside it.
A hatchet.
A scented candle.
A little clay cat.
A Coleman lantern.
A can of tomato soup, unopened.
A beer mug.
I wasn't always a killer or a thief. For
years I just drifted around, carefree in
my stupidity. I gravitated to out of the
way dives where, for five bucks, I'd
swallow a beer mug, or a cue ball, or, as
noted, an unopened can of soup.
And then there was Tijuana.

Chapter Eight
Kissing the Grim Reaper

SUNDAY WRINKLED HER NOSE as she crept back toward wakefulness. What was that smell?

She opened one eye. Her nose was practically jammed into a man's armpit. She opened her other eye. Why was she sleeping on someone else's arm? And why was she cold? Why did her bones ache?

Right, right, right. She'd fallen asleep with Pit Geek. They'd crash landed in an ice-cold lake then fallen asleep on a rug. At some point, he'd removed his leather jacket and draped it over them. Given that it was sopping wet that had done more to chill them than warm them. Her only other blanket was a canvas banner.

She sat up. Pit was snoring. His shirtsleeve had a dark stain where she'd drooled on his arm. She rubbed her eyes. Daylight streamed through gaps in the shutters covering the windows. Dust danced in the sunbeams gleaming on the pine floors. She wrapped the banner around her to fight the chill.

She knew she could solve the problem of the cold in a heartbeat.

Except she couldn't. Something bad had happened to her last night. She'd never pushed her power so far, never tried anything as ambitious as melting an entire mountain. At first, letting go like that had been liberating. But later, when she'd cooled down to pick up Pit, she'd felt as if all her life's energy was draining out of her. Ordinarily, using her powers required concentration, but wasn't physically demanding. Her father had said that the heat and light she commanded weren't coming out of her, but from the sun. It was free energy, channeled through the tiny wormholes she summoned into existence around her.

He'd never said where the energy to open the wormholes came from.

She rubbed her arms. Her bones felt like they were full of needles. Her pale and bloodless skin was covered in goose bumps.

She'd died last night.

She remembered the truck tire catching her in the gut. Remembered the way her ribs had snapped and knifed into her lungs. Her mind went black at the moment she fell toward the trees, but then there was a vivid image she couldn't shake. She'd opened her eyes while she was on the ground. She couldn't move her legs, and she couldn't summon her fire, and she was coughing, and coughing, and drops of blood were spattering her eyes.

A black cloud had moved in from the edges of her vision and she'd stopped coughing. Everything had gone quiet, and then she'd been dead.

Now she was alive.

She looked at Pit. His broken nose had popped back out, and was almost back to normal. He was still missing a hand, though the stump had healed over with new pink flesh. She couldn't bring herself to look at his mangled groin.

He'd had the regeneration ray. He'd used it on her instead of fixing himself. Would she have done the same?

She stood up, careful not to wake him. Maybe he was just used to being hurt. The whole time she'd known him, he'd always been healing from some new bullet hole, or worse things. And he did heal quickly. It was one of his powers. He didn't need the ray. He just needed time. He'd only used the ray on her because he needed her help to escape Servant. It was a simple logical strategy.

Or maybe he . . . maybe he actually cared for her.

She walked from window to window, peering through the gaps in the shutters. There was mist over the lake. Nothing but trees on the other side of the water. She could barely see the front porch of the next cabin over from the window on the side wall. That was probably the cabin with the king sized beds covered with goose-down comforters.

If Pit cared for her, it was just a sex thing. He was constantly making his clumsy advances, passing them off as jokes, but she knew that he wanted her. Maybe he thought by saving her life she'd be so indebted to him that she'd let him paw and slobber over her to satisfy his animalistic male craving to dominate her.

She sighed.

It was her father who'd been a rapist. Maybe it was time to stop projecting that trait onto all men. She'd just wrapped her nude body across Pit Geek like he was her personal body pillow and he hadn't laid a finger on her.

Maybe he was a decent guy deep down. Yes, he was dumb, and crude, and clueless, but he seemed comfortable in his own skin in a way she'd never been.

Maybe. . . .

Maybe she didn't hate all mankind.

She walked over to him. She nudged his cheek with her ice-cold toe.

"Wake up," she said.

Pit kept his eyes closed and rolled over.

She put her toe in his ear and wiggled it. "Wake up."

He opened his eyes and rolled onto his back. He stared up her long legs to where they disappeared under the wrap of the banner. He looked disoriented for about half a minute, then he grinned as his eyes fixed on her face. "Ain't this a fine way to start the day," he said.

"A better way to start the day would be with coffee," she said. "And some clothes. And some transportation. And some clue as to where the hell we are."

"West Virginia," he said. "Maybe Ohio. Or Kentucky."

"I guess it doesn't matter," she said.

"Naw," he said. "Banks are the same no matter where we rob 'em."

"We're done robbing banks," she said.

He propped himself up on his right elbow. He stared at the stump of his left hand, looking puzzled. "We must have had one wild night."

"You don't remember?" she asked.

He sat up, scratching the back of his head. Then he carefully touched his nose, and finding it improved, shoved his finger into it and began to dig out big black globs of dried blood. "Yeah, I remember now," he said. "Supercops. It just takes my brain a while to get going some mornings."

"Mine too," she said. "Let's break into the rest of the cabins and see if there's a mess hall."

"What are we going to rob?" he asked.

"The mess hall?" she answered, not understanding his question.

"I mean, what are we robbing if we're not robbing banks?"

"Nothing," she said. "I've decided you're right. We'll go to Pangea. We'll retire and spend the rest of our lives drinking banana daiquiris."

"You think we've got enough?"

"By my count you've got about eighty million dollars swimming around in that mysterious gut of yours, and that's just the cash. We'll be all right."

Pit nodded. "What changed your mind?"

"It's a different game, if superheroes are back," she said. "I don't want to play any more."

He furrowed his brow. "You scared? 'Cause by my scorecard, we licked them pretty good."

"I'm not scared," she said, turning her face back to the window so he wouldn't be able to see her eyes. "But the war is over. We've got all the money we'll need to buy a little peace and quiet. I just don't have anything left worth fighting for."

This was answered with silence. She turned back toward Pit, and found he had his hand crammed deep into his mouth. He produced the regeneration ray a few seconds later.

He aimed it at his left hand and pulled the trigger. In under a minute, he was wiggling fresh fingers.

He rose and dropped his pants. He squatted, looking awkward as he tried to aim the gun at the affected area. She sighed.

"Give me that."

He handed her the gun.

"Sit there," she said, pointing to the hearth of the fireplace, which was raised off the floor about a foot.

He did so.

She crouched before him and pushed his knees apart. She grimaced.

"Bad?" he asked.

"What did he use on you? A chainsaw?"

"I think it was his toenails. Sort of mutified."

She set her jaw and breathed through her nose. He'd brought her back from the dead. She at least owed him the fortitude not to turn away from his mangled manhood. She took aim and pulled the trigger. The gun began to scan. It ran through all of its normal commands, but introduced a new one: "Removing foreign matter." Suddenly small dark pins, rings, and balls began to ooze from his flesh and drop onto the stone hearth, making soft clicking sounds as they bounced.

"What the hell?" she asked.

"Damned if I know," he said.

Half a minute later, the job was finished. Pit had a fresh new pair of hairless testicles and his penis seemed intent to prove its repaired blood flow by sporting a rather impressive erection. Of course, Sunday might have been easily impressed. She didn't have much to judge these things by. She felt an almost overwhelming urge to reach out and measure this part of his anatomy by comparing it to her hand size, but she was absolutely certain this would be misinterpreted.

She said nothing.

Pit wisely acted as if he didn't notice anything out of the ordinary about the situation. Instead, he picked up some of the small metal bits that had fallen from him. He stared at them, and suddenly she could see a spark in his eyes.

"You remember something?"

"Maybe," he said.

"What?"

"I . . . I don't know where it was. Down south somewhere, maybe. I remember there was a two-lane road, and right beside one another, a bar, a tattoo parlor, a Holiness church, and a graveyard, all lined up in front of a couple of acres of old mobile homes."

"What's that got to do with those?" She nodded toward the fragments.

"A woman ran the tattoo parlor. Wendy? Cindy? Candy? We met at the bar. She was just getting started in the tattoo business. I told her she could practice on me. She used to draw all kinds of designs on me. A week later, they'd just fade away, like my body thought they were just another injury. She also did piercing. I think my body absorbed some of them."

Sunday furrowed her brow. "You let someone shove metal into your genitals?"

"She was real nice to me," said Pit, with a shrug.

"But you don't remember her name?"

"I don't remember my name."

"So what happened to her?"

Pit said nothing. His eyes went vacant, like he was searching through all the little film loops in his brain, trying to find one that answered her question. He shook his head and grabbed his pants. He looked at the bloodied crotch.

"Guess I should wash these," he said.

"Or burn 'em," she said.

"It was cancer," he said. "Cancer's what happened to her."

"Oh," she said.

"She'd been sick before I met her. Breast cancer. She'd tattooed over the two long scars on her chest. Lightning bolts. Said she had power over death."

He shook his head. "She was the skinniest woman you ever seen. Then the cancer came back. Chemo made all her hair fall out, even her pubes, even her eyebrows. Her skin was so smooth and soft. She didn't feel much like going out, so we'd just lie around in bed, holding each other, the hours rolling by. I'd try to cheer her up. Tell her she was beautiful as her hair fell out and her face turned slowly into a skull. 'My cancer beauty,' I called her."

He pulled on his pants. "And then she got really sick." He

tucked his still erect penis up against his belly. "And then she died."

"I'm sorry," said Sunday.

"Aw, it's nothing," he said, shrugging. "Everyone dies. Everyone."

"You don't."

"Yeah," he said. "I do. A little every day. You ain't looking at a living man. You're looking at a corpse too stupid to call it quits."

"You keep saying you're stupid," she said, brushing her hair back from her face, "but the more I listen to you, the more I suspect you're secretly kind of smart."

"That's just my dumbness rubbing off on you," he said.

"If so, I wish more of you were rubbing off on me."

Pit looked down at his jeans, at his still noticeable erection. "Are you . . . are you saying . . ."

"No!" she said, feeling her cheeks flush. "God no. I'm saying that you've got this . . . this quiet wisdom about you. A calmness. You seem . . . centered. I'd like to learn how you get there."

"Brain damage, mostly," he said.

THE NEXT CABIN over turned out to be a chapel. In a room behind the altar there was a small kitchen and, praise the Lord, a coffee maker and an unopened vacuum pack of Starbucks coffee. Because the Lord was kind, water ran when they opened the tap. They plugged the pot in. Because the Lord was cruel, there was no electricity. Pit flipped a few switches.

Nothing.

"I bet there's a breaker box," she said. "Check outside."

"Can't you heat the water with your powers?"

She froze. It was a very simple question.

For a brain-damaged freak, he picked up instantly that something was wrong.

"Has something happened to your powers?"

"What?" she said. "No. Why would you think that?"

"Well, you ain't glowed even a little bit since we climbed out of the lake. Usually by this time of day, you've lit up a time or two."

"Usually by this time of day, I've had coffee," she said.

"You need coffee to use your powers?" he said. "That seems like some kind of weakness."

"Some kind, yeah," she said. "Look, it's nothing big. I used a lot of power last night. It's left me feeling a little . . . unsteady. I need to . . . if the heroes show back up, I need to save my strength."

Pit leaned back against the sink, staring at her.

"What?" she asked.

"The first time I met you, you had trouble turning your powers on."

"That was ten years ago," she said. "I was just a little girl."

"You were afraid of losing control."

"What are you now? My dad?"

"You still touch yourself?"

"Pit!" she said. "What's gotten into you? And how can you possibly know about that?"

"Monday told me before I ever met you that was how you found out about your powers. Maybe I got a dirty mind, but it's a memory that stuck with me."

"What I do or don't do with my body is none of your business." She went the tap and filled the carafe with water, then dumped in a random amount of coffee. She'd do this without electricity. Where the hell did Pit get off asking something like that?

She cradled the pitcher between her palms. She took a deep, slow breath. All she had to do was let out a little heat. Very little. Too much and she'd blow up the pot. She imagined shards of glass flying everywhere. She visualized a sliver sinking into her eye, driving into her brain.

The water stayed cold.

"You can't do it," said Pit.

"I just don't want coffee all that badly," she said, putting the carafe down on the counter. "It wouldn't taste right without it dripping through a filter."

"Sure it would," he said, eyeing the grounds in the water. "That there's cowboy coffee!"

She stared at her hands. All she needed to do to get past this was just make a little ball of light in her palm. Just something the size of a marble.

Nothing.

Pit said, "Looks like we're gonna have to go into town for some java."

She shook her head.

"We should stay here," she said.

"Someone will find us here."

She nodded. "I know. So. I should stay here. You should go."

"That don't make sense," he said.

"I can't turn my powers on," she whispered.

"You mean I was right?" He scratched his head. "Man, I oughta write this down."

"What you oughta do is go," she said. "Right now, I'm a liability. Leave me my half of the money and go on. If I get my powers back, I'll meet you in Pangea."

Pit shook his head. "Naw, we're a team. We go together."

"A team is only as strong as its weakest link," she said.

"You're thinking of a chain," he said. "And yesterday you melted a mountain while I coasted down a burning road in a crippled truck. Who was the weak link then? You've stood by me. I'll stand by you."

She crossed her arms. "You don't understand." She felt on the verge of tears. "I died. I died! And, using my powers last night . . . it hurt! When I was powering down it felt . . . it felt like I was being hollowed out. The pain was . . . it made me . . . I don't want to die, Pit. I'm not like you. I can't just shrug this shit off."

"Then don't shrug it off," he said. "Wrap both arms around the idea and pull it close."

"Embrace dying?"

"Death is like a mean dog. You show fear and it's gonna chase you. But you run at it growling, and it backs off."

"I saw you try that trick in Toronto eight years ago," she said.

"You got bit!"

"But I bit him back. Look, you gotta stare the Grim Reaper straight in the eye, grab him by his hood and plant a big one on his bony chin. If it's your time, he'll kiss you back. If not, you're gonna make him more scared of you than you are of him."

She rubbed her arms, thinking about what he said. She was as cold as she'd ever been, and her bones still hurt. If she'd ever felt more afraid, she couldn't remember when. But she took some degree of comfort that Pit was going to stick around.

"You look cold," he said.

"It's freezing!" she said, shivering. "Wasn't it hot yesterday? Where's global warming when you really need it?"

Pit took off his biker jacket and held it out to her. "I'd have given it to you sooner if I'd known you couldn't make yourself hot no more," he said, sounding sincerely apologetic.

She looked at the jacket like he was handing her a bomb.

"Something wrong?" he asked. "It smell bad?"

She took the jacket. "It smells fine." The leather was still damp, but it was warm from his body heat. She said, "You keep being kind to me. Kindness messes with every assumption I hold about humanity."

"It ain't no sure thing that I'm human," he said.

She slipped her arms into the sleeves. Then, for the first time in her adult life, she couldn't help herself. She hugged him. He held his hands out awkwardly to the side.

"Whatever you are," she whispered, "the world needs more like you."

He carefully wrapped his arms around her. He patted her back, as if she needed comfort.

But what if she didn't need comfort?

She tilted her face toward his. He stared into her eyes, looking confused. She held his gaze. His eyes were brown, the irises looking almost like they'd been carved and polished from some rare wood.

"You, uh," he said. "You . . . got nice eyes. You could, uh, you could be a model?"

"You really should just give up on sweet talk," she said,

standing on her tiptoes.

He took the hint and kissed her.

He hugged her even tighter. She ran her fingers up his neck and mussed with his curls.

Embrace death, he'd said. *Run straight towards it.*

She moved her hand toward his crotch. Since the Grim Reaper wasn't around, she chose to grab hold of her second worse fear. She found his fly and toyed with it. He moved from her mouth to nibble on her ears. The sensation was electric.

"I don't touch myself," she whispered in his ear as he nibbled on her neck. "I haven't come since I was fifteen. The second I found out Rex Monday could watch anything I did, I swore off sex. I'm still a virgin."

Pit put his hands under her butt and lifted her onto the counter. He tore away the cloth banner under her leather jacket and pressed his mouth between her breasts. Then his tongue found her nipple. She gasped, then tilted her head back and groaned as heat flooded her body.

His rough fingers slipped between her thighs. She instinctively closed her legs, trapping his hand. There was no need to rush this. Kissing and a little fondling were enough for now, weren't they? Pit didn't push. He waited patiently, his hand hot against her smooth skin. Caution and timidity were such human traits. Sunday knew that thinking too much had once kept her from reaching the sky. If she was going to fly again, she had to let go of all doubt and hesitation. Drawing a breath, she spread her knees apart.

She gasped as his fingers slipped slowly along her flesh. Her fears vanished beneath a wave of pleasure.

The paint began to peel from the kitchen walls. Soon, the air smelled of burning coffee as the last of the water boiled away.

Clean water is hard to find. The loose stuff drifts around in little spheres, most no bigger than ball bearings. I found an orb the size of a baseball last week and felt like I'd found gold. Except, gold's easy to find. Bars, coins, rings, chains and sometimes little chewed up nuggets.

Useless.

If I could melt it all down I'd have enough to build a throne. I'd be Midas, king of this world.

Rex mundi.

Dying of thirst.

Why didn't I drink more water?

Chapter Nine
Homes of the Heroes

AP WANTED TO BE DISCRETE. He couldn't just ask Simpson to cut and paste him into Detroit. Ap had no ties at all to the city, no reason to go there. If it was true that Servant had once been the meta-human drug lord known as Ogre, how high did the secret go? Did Simpson know? Did Katrina Knowbokov, who bankrolled the whole operation? Whose toes was he stepping on by pursuing the truth?

The irony was, he had a damn teleportation belt, and the one thing the geniuses here hadn't figured out how to do was to make it teleport him anywhere. Not that he was ungrateful. The restore application had worked beautifully, resetting his body to the exact condition it had been a week ago, when he'd done his last back up scan. From now on he was doing those scans daily.

In the end he'd had Simpson send him to Chicago. He'd mentioned a few touristy things he planned to do with his time off. Simpson seemed to buy the cover story. Unlike comic book heroes who always seemed to work pro bono, members of the Covenant were paid a generous salary, so he'd made reservations at the Peninsula Chicago, the fanciest hotel he'd ever stayed at, not that he intended to actually stay there. Instead, he checked in, removed the space machine transponder unit from his belt, and plugged it into the bathroom outlet to charge. He put his cell phone into the same outlet. Without these, he was no longer transmitting real time data revealing his location. He now had his privacy, but he was also working without a safety net. He didn't even have an internet connection. He was so used to the streams of data in his retinal display that he felt off balance, half-blind and stupid, as he went down to the lobby to meet the courier bringing him his rental car.

Once he got behind the wheel, the sensation was even worse. He'd never driven before he got dematerialized. He'd gotten his drivers license only a month ago, and this had been with his retinal display providing every answer on the written test. His actual hours logged behind a wheel were less than twenty, and this mostly around Katrina Knowbokov's private island, where there were fewer than ten cars, total.

So, to pull out into Chicago traffic and drive seven hours down congested interstates to reach Detroit was a bit outside his comfort zone, to say the least. By the time he arrived at his destination, he felt as burned out and rattled as he had after his confrontation with Pit Geek.

The Detroit Cube was in the middle of a nice park, surrounded by older homes that had been gentrified. Just a decade ago, this had been the worst part of town, a little feudal kingdom where Ogre's gang had been the only law. But, after Rail Blade had trapped and presumably killed Ogre in a battle that flattened seven blocks of rat-infested hovels, the Knowbokov foundation had given the city grants to build a park around the thirty foot steel cube. The rusted monument seemed to speak of Detroit's industrial past. There were uglier works of municipal art than this.

The park was nearly empty by the time Ap arrived. It was windy and cold and right on the edge of sunset. Except for a bundled up man walking his dog, no one else was anywhere near the cube.

Since he had no internet, Ap had already downloaded the three programs he wanted to try into his belt.

"Magnavision mode," he said. Then he stuck a two-pound molybdenum magnet on the south face of the cube and walked around to the north. The rust brown cube now glowed green in his altered eyes. In theory, the earth's own magnetic field flowing would interfere with the magnet on the far side and his retinas would be able to spot anomalies. And, he could see, very, very faintly, a blob near the center of the cube. But what did that mean? Was he looking at a dead man-monster? Or only a hollow space?

"Well, that didn't work," he said, walking back to the magnet. He tried to pull it off. It may as well have been welded on.

"Double density mode," he said. His arms and chest burned as the muscle fibers packed within them thickened. Even with the added strength, he had to put his shoulder against the cube for leverage as he pried the magnet free.

Ap looked around, making certain no one had watched his struggles. Satisfied that he was alone, he whispered, "Ultrasound mode."

Suddenly, he heard the babble of every conversation taking place in the houses surrounding the park. He heard the *chuff chuff chuff* of the dog walker's pants legs rubbing together from a hundred yards away. From every direction came the rumble of traffic.

HE WAS GRATEFUL there was no one near enough to see him since he now had four ears. The two he'd been born with were now long, stretched out, and forward facing. Two smaller ones thrust up from his temples like horns. He pressed his face to the cube and rapped it with his knuckles.

It wasn't quite right to say that he could see the middle of the cube. His mind was flooded with sensory data that he didn't possess the vocabulary to describe. It was nothing like hospital ultrasounds, where a computer converted sound into light. But what he heard intrigued him. If he understood the vibration patterns, the middle of the cube was hollow. What's more, there was a shaft down from the center extending into the ground.

"End ultrasound mode," he said.

He shoved his hands into his jacket pocket and pulled up his hood. The sun had gone down, and the wind was knifing right through him. He wandered around the park until he found a manhole cover. If he'd been online, he could have walked into the cube in his ghost mode. But he couldn't do it without GPS. The second he stepped into the cube he'd be completely blind.

If he stumbled around lost for too long in solid steel, he'd suffocate. Hell, even if he had been online, his GPS signal would almost certainly be cut off the second he stepped inside. So, he'd have to do this the hard way.

In double density mode, he shoved his fingers into the manhole cover and pulled it aside. A dank smell of rot wafted up from the hole. Ap paused. What was he really expecting to learn by going down there?

He hadn't come all this way to turn back now. Activating the LED flashlight on his belt buckle, he climbed down the ladder, into a concrete tunnel about six feet high and eight feet across. To his relief, the drain was dry save for a trickle of moist sludge at the very center.

The shaft ran on a course that led it under the cube. He followed it, and right where he judged the center of the cube to be, he found that the roof was a different color than the rest of the tunnel. It wasn't exactly new, but it was definitely newer than the surrounding walls.

He switched to camcorder mode and began to record the areas of the tunnel where new concrete met old. It wasn't the most exciting evidence he could have collected, but he felt like he should leave with at least something.

Satisfied he'd done all he could, Ap turned back toward the entrance.

The tunnel suddenly turned bright as his belt light reflected against something pure white.

Ap started to speak, but a beefy hand clamped over his mouth and picked him up, slamming him back into the concrete wall. Servant stood before him, his eyes narrowed into little slits.

"So you know the truth," said Servant. "Happy?"

Ap couldn't answer.

"Ogre was a killer," said Servant. "Worse than a killer. He would have made a skinny thing like you into his bitch. You'd have begged for death when he was done with you."

Ap reached for his belt. Apparently, Servant was under the impression that Ap could only activate his powers with voice commands. While that was convenient in the heat of battle, he also had a keypad on his belt, and his best modes saved as hotkeys.

Servant suddenly lurched forward, his hand hitting concrete, as Ap entered ghost mode.

"I've read all about you," Ap said. "You're as bad as the people we're hunting. Worse!"

"Pit Geek and Sundancer are terrorists trying to bring down civilization," said Servant. "I hardly think running a gang makes me worse. If anything, the drug trade is a celebration of capitalism."

"Your gang wars killed hundreds. Most of them kids! And who knows how many thousands of people died from the poison you were peddling?"

"The only reason we were selling drugs is that weak little punks like you were willing to get on your knees in front of a stranger to get the money to pay us for another hit. You can't condemn the supply when you were part of the demand."

"I never killed anyone," said Ap.

"Everyone kills somebody," said Servant. "You think your parents weren't dying knowing what you were doing out there on the streets?"

"This isn't about me," said Ap. "My record's clean. As far as the state is concerned, I've paid my debts."

"And you think I haven't paid for my crimes?" asked Servant. "Rail Blade locked me in a metal cube for three damn months! There's no prison in the world where a man gets locked up so he can't move, can't see, can't breathe or shit or piss. I thought I was dead. I thought I was in hell! Trapped with nothing but memories, with all my rage and mental violence turned against my own soul. I thought I'd been in hell for centuries when Rail Blade yanked me out so her dad could autopsy me. They were both surprised when I woke up." He shook his head, like he was shaking away bad memories. "I was too."

"Fine," said Ap. "You had three bad months. If you'd ever been put on trial, you'd have been executed. Three months is a joke."

"I didn't find it funny," said Servant. He looked up at the

ceiling, his eyes haunted as he gazed at his former tomb. "I meant what I said about thinking I was in hell. My mother was a good woman. Used to take me to church. I can't blame her for not making sure I understood the consequences of my actions. I'd been warned about hell, told to repent and give my life to Jesus. I knew right from wrong."

He looked Ap squarely in the face and said, "I know you don't believe me, but Ogre really did die in that cube. The person that woke up under Dr. Know's scalpel was a new man. Having been given a taste of hell, I committed my life to Jesus. Rail Blade wasn't happy, but Dr. Know said he believed in second chances. I was just a kid, then, only thirteen."

"You were only thirteen when you ran the most feared gang in Detroit?"

Servant shrugged. "I was big for my age. Big and stupid. Dr. Know arranged for me to get back in school. It wasn't easy catching up, but I made it through high school. I was in my second year of college before Katrina Knowbokov approached me about joining the Covenant. This is my chance to make up for the bad things I did in my old life."

Ap sighed. "Fine. I guess . . . I understand second chances."

"Then we're cool?" asked Servant.

"For now," said Ap. "I probably would have taken this better if you'd just trusted me from the start and not turned this into some kind of mystery."

"Do you really think the world would accept me if they knew my past?"

"Well," said Ap. "Probably not."

"What if they knew yours?"

Ap crossed his arms. "If stuff comes out, I'll deal with it."

"You're on a good team for keeping secrets," said Servant. "Mrs. Knowbokov is pretty good at stopping reporters who snoop around into our real identities."

"How does she stop it?"

"I kill most of them," said Servant.

Ap froze.

"That's a joke," said the big man. "The boss lady is richer than

Oprah. She buys people's silence."

"Right," said Ap.

"So, you drove here?" said Servant.

"Yeah," said Ap. "It was kind of a nightmare."

"I love driving," said Servant. "You want a partner for a road trip back to Chicago?"

"Why not?" said Ap. He began walking back up the tunnel toward the manhole cover. His thoughts were churning. Servant seemed sincere. And Ap was committed to the belief that people could turn their lives around. The one thing that Ap still worried about was that Servant seemed to crediting God for his conversion. Ap didn't believe in God. He'd changed because he'd found the strength inside himself to change. Servant had changed to try to get into the good graces of a mythical being. Would his conversion hold if something shook his faith?

PIT AND SUNDAY had come to L.A. since the Pangeans had an embassy here, but Pit had a second agenda. They were a day early for their meeting. They'd made good time across the desert in their stolen Sebring. They'd put the top down and Sunday had spent most of the trip stretched out with her seat back, her eyes shielded by a comically large pair of sunglasses, lightly snoring. They'd stolen new clothes from a Goodwill in Kentucky. Sunday had picked up the garish pink sunglasses and asked, "Who'd wear something like this?" She'd popped them on her face. "They look like something a female fugitive in a bad movie would wear to hide her identity." She'd worn them pretty much non-stop since they'd been on the road.

It wasn't just the glasses that made her look like a different woman. Despite her brief fling as a biker in a leather halter-top, for most of the years Pit had known Sunday, she'd dressed conservatively. She didn't show a lot of skin and usually wore muted colors. She was now dressed in a short pink sundress with spaghetti strap shoulders. Her legs were mostly bare.

"I really need to even up the color with a tan," she'd explained.

Pit wondered if she was trying to dress like the kind of woman that Pit used to associate with. He wanted to tell her it wasn't necessary, but, on the other hand, he was the last person on earth to tell anyone anything about clothes.

He was a little worried about how much she was sleeping. Admittedly, he was keeping her up half the night. She had good reason to be worn out. But ever since he'd brought her back to life, she'd been sleeping at least twelve hours a day. She seemed okay when she was awake, and she said she'd never felt better in her life, but he wondered if she was keeping something from him.

Right now, however, she was awake. They were driving around Hollywood with a black and white Xeroxed map with fancy letters at the top that read, "Homes of the Heroes of the Old West." On the back was a list of about a hundred names. Luckily, it wasn't just heroes on the list. Frank Macey, the Stick-Em-Up Kid, was number 48.

They pulled up in front of a squat beige bungalow in a run-down neighborhood.

"914," said Sunday, squinting at the numbers on the door. "This is it."

Pit stared at the small house. There was a wooden fence hiding the back yard. A few sunflowers peeked over the top.

"Look familiar?" she asked.

It did look familiar. But it looked familiar because they'd stopped at a Kinko's in Lexington and read everything on the internet about Frank Macey. Pit was pretty sure there'd been a black and white photo of Macey standing in front of this house.

He knew, without knowing why he knew, that the house had once been painted the same yellow as the sunflowers. There hadn't been a fence. The living room had wooden floors and there had been a big black and white rug. He remembered . . . he remembered the filthy beige tiles of a bathroom covered with broken mirror shards, reflecting fragments of his face back at him.

Had he lived here?

Was he Frank Macey? The kid in the red tights had been right.

With his new face, he was a dead ringer for the actor. Macey had been a recurring bad guy in the *Dallas Smith, Texas Ranger* franchise. He'd appeared in over thirty films. But the series ended in 1942, when the actor who played Dallas Smith had joined the army and died handling a live hand-grenade before he ever got out of boot camp. Macey had appeared in a handful of films after that, never again in a western, but always playing a gangster or some other kind of thug. He'd also gained a reputation for showing up drunk.

Macey had wound up working for the L.A. sanitation department, driving a garbage truck.

And in 1956, both Macey and the truck had simply vanished.

Pit's earliest memories bubbled up at the tail end of the 1950s.

"I said, look familiar?" Sunday asked after he'd stared in silence at the house for two minutes.

"Naw," he whispered. "I mean, yeah, a little. But not what I was wantin'. No flood of memories. I thought I'd feel like I was waking up."

Sunday leaned back in her seat. "I haven't felt wide awake in three days," she said.

"You've been sleeping a lot."

"It's your fault," she said. "You keep me up half the night. Every muscle in my body is sore."

"That just means we're doing it right."

"I still think not sleeping is my problem. When you finally do settle down, you steal the covers."

"We're lucky I ain't eaten one yet."

"You've eaten blankets?"

"Used to eat all kinds of stuff when I was sleeping. Ain't done it in years, though. Once I dreamed I was eating a big marshmallow. When I woke up my pillow was gone."

Sunday groaned. "That joke stopped being funny in kindergarten."

Pit scratched his head. "What joke?"

I woke up on the side of the highway in
the middle of the desert. The sun was
beating down on me something fierce.
There was an ambulance parked next to me,
and a man in a tan uniform leaning over
me, his hands pressed against my neck.
"You just lie still," he said.
I looked around. There was a highway
patrol car behind the ambulance, its
lights flashing. A cop was standing at
the open door of the ambulance, talking
to another medic.
"Where am I?" I asked. The ground around
me was all covered in trash and twisted
metal. Big purple chunks of what looked
like rotten meat were scattered through
the debris. The air smelled like a dump.
"You're about twenty miles outside of
Las Vegas," the medic said, as he pointed
a small flashlight at my eyes. "You been
drinking?
"I don't remember," I said. "What
happened?"
"We were wondering the same thing."
"So hot," I said, putting my hands over
my eyes to block the sun. I tried to sit
up. The man helped me. My clothes were
shredded, like I'd been chewed in the
teeth of a giant machine, but my skin
didn't even have a scratch.
The medic held a green canteen to my
lips. "Have some water," he said.
I opened my mouth. He suddenly toppled
over, his arm gone up to his shoulder. He
fell to the ground in shock and began to
bleed out.

"Tommy!" the other medic screamed, running toward his partner.

"What just happened?" I asked. But when I opened my mouth, the scraps of garbage around me began to swirl, rising in a tornado, the tip of the vortex aimed right at my mouth.

The second medic stumbled and slipped as he saw this. His right foot fell into the edge of the swirling trash.

In terror, I opened my mouth even wider as I screamed. His fingers clawed at the ground as the lower half of his body began to stretch like strands of spaghetti.

Not knowing what to do, I closed my mouth. The man's legs vanished. He didn't live but a second or two after that.

The cop emptied his pistol in me as I staggered toward him, desperate for help, completely out of my mind with panic. One of his bullets caught me in the left cheek and wound up in my inner ear, leaving me with the worst vertigo imaginable. I fell against him and his face twisted into an unrecognizable spiral of flesh. I locked my jaw shut and the front half of his skull vanished, revealing the gray-pink cauliflower of his brain.

Despite myself, I screamed again.

I found the rear door of an old ambulance in the rubble today.

I think of all those years I wandered around, longing for memories, hungry to recall what had happened the day before, let along the month before, or the year before.

If only I'd known what a gift my forgetfulness was.

Chapter Ten
No Human Casualties

PIT PARKED on the fifth floor of the mall parking deck. It was lunchtime and the place was packed. He and Sunday rode the elevator down to the second floor, where there was a walkway to the food court. The walkway was crammed with people.

"Look at them," said Sunday, sounding contemptuous. She shook her head.

"Look at who?" he asked.

"All these people!" she said. "My father said that the true criminals of the world got away with their crimes by providing the masses with bread and circuses. Crimes of the highest magnitude can take place in plain sight as long as the citizens have stores full of flashy goods and easy credit to buy whatever they've been brainwashed to want."

"What crimes?" Pit asked, through he regretted asking the second the words left his lips.

Sunday brandished a fist. "The greatest theft of all is the theft of minds! From birth, these people are programmed by televised propaganda until they believe the surest path to joy and fulfillment is to buy the right toilet paper and wear the right brand of jeans. They can never stop and think about the higher purpose of life because they're distracted from cradle to grave by the lowest common denominator types of entertainment."

"What if there ain't no higher purpose?"

Sunday paused on the enclosed walkway, pressing her hand against the glass as she stared out at the crowded street below. "The world could be changed into Utopia if these people pooled their intellects to pursue grand goals. Instead, they spend their days thinking of how much they want their next can of addictive soda. They spend their evenings laughing at fart jokes. They believe this to be the pinnacle of the human condition."

Pit scratched his chin. It probably looked like he was thinking about what she was saying. In reality, his face itched. His stubble was thick and prickly. He'd tried to keep his new face cleanly shaved, but it was more work than it was really worth. He'd never liked looking at himself in a mirror. He'd always felt like he was looking at a stranger. Shaving made him remember how much he didn't remember.

Earlier in the day, Sunday had made a phone call to the Pangean embassy and spoken to Dr. Cheetah. He'd advised against coming to the embassy directly. The roads around the property were under heavy surveillance. Instead, they were meeting at the food court of a busy mall, where the sheer number of bodies would help them hide in plain site. Pit thought a super-intelligent chimpanzee was going to stand out pretty much anywhere they met, but he didn't have a better place in mind.

The food court was bigger than some of the small towns they'd spent the last few weeks driving through. The place was full of trees and flowers. Television screens showing advertisements and news feeds were spread liberally among the branches. He braced himself for a speech from Sunday about how trying to make the indoors look like the outdoors was some subtle evil meant to pacify the masses, but, if she was thinking it, she let it slide.

Instead, her eyes focused on a Muslim woman in a full veil sitting in a wheelchair at a table dead center of the food court. A beefy black man in teal medical scrubs stood behind her, staring stone faced at Sunday and Pit as they drew nearer.

The woman in the veil held up her gloved hand and motioned for Pit and Sunday to have a seat. Sunday sat first, and said, "Thank you for meeting us on such short notice, Dr. Cheetah."

"Think nothing of it," said Dr. Cheetah. The voice had a buzz like an electric razor beneath it. He'd heard the chimps needed mechanical assistance to speak verbal languages. The voice had a masculine depth to it. Pit realized he wasn't certain if Dr. Cheetah was male or female. The chimp continued, "We owe an immeasurable debt to your father. When one of his surviving children contacts us, the least we can do is afford her the opportunity to speak with us."

"His only surviving child at this point," said Sunday. "The Panic and Baby Gun are dead."

"Don't forget Ogre," said Dr. Cheetah.

"Was Ogre my father's child?" asked Sunday, sounding surprised.

"I reviewed your father's genetics catalogue personally," said Dr. Cheetah.

"He never told me," she said. Then, she leaned back in her chair and waved her hand dismissively. "In any case, Rail Blade killed him years ago."

"Oh dear," said Dr. Cheetah. "You've been in hiding many years. I take it your access to information was limited."

"Extremely limited," said Sunday. "The only message I've gotten from my father in seven years was a note a few weeks ago telling me the war was over."

"The note couldn't have come from your father," said Dr. Cheetah. "He was killed several years ago. I thought you knew. I'm sorry to be the bearer of this news."

Sunday looked stunned. She sagged into her chair, going silent. One of her hands was still on the table and Dr. Cheetah reached out and clasped her hand in sympathy.

Pit saw the ape's eyes shift under the veil to stare at his face.

Dr. Cheetah said, "You appear skeptical, Mr. Geek."

Pit shrugged. "Naw. I'm just sitting here trying to figure out if you're a boy monkey or a girl monkey."

"Chimps aren't monkeys," Dr. Cheetah said, curtly. "I'm male; it's just convenient that your species has a culture where one sex only appears in public with their bodies completely covered. It makes moving about in the city more convenient for me."

Sunday pulled her hand free of Dr. Cheetah's grasp. "How do you know he's dead? Did you see the body?"

"No," said Dr. Cheetah. "We learned it through contacts at the Knowbokov Foundation."

"Then all you have are rumors. The Knowbokov's were my father's enemies. They could be spreading lies, or he could be fooling them into thinking he's dead."

"Perhaps this is so," Dr. Cheetah said. "My apologies if I've passed along unverified information."

"In any case, we've not arranged this meeting to exchange gossip or rumors. We've come to discuss business."

"I've been following your recent adventures with great interest," said Dr. Cheetah. "After so long in hiding, you've disturbed the status quo greatly. The rise of this new team of heroes is an unpleasant development."

"Unpleasant for us," said Pit. "What's it to you?"

"The public at large is extremely uncomfortable with the whole notion of Pangea. While the United States government has granted us official recognition, the airwaves are filled with loud voices denouncing us as inhuman abominations and clamoring for our destruction. It's the human way to hate those who are different. Now that superhumans are once more openly flying over their heads, the resentment of the general public against so-called 'freaks of science' is further inflamed. But it is difficult to turn this hatred into violence against superheroes. The heroes are, after all, supremely suited to withstand acts of aggression. We Pangeans are few in number. We do not fly, nor can we lift tanks above our heads. Our seeming weakness makes us tempting targets."

"Your people do command my father's army of killbots," said Sunday.

"That provides some measure of deterrence, yes. But we are also a struggling young country. We're vulnerable to economic sanctions in a way that superhumans are not."

Sunday leaned forward. She said, softly, "We can help with the economics."

"So you can," said Dr. Cheetah.

"Let's cut to the chase," said Sunday. "We need a sanctuary. Right now, there's no country in the world that would give us safe harbor, at least none with a decent standard of living. I don't want to hide in some desert cave the rest of my life. We're wealthy people. We'd like to spend this money someplace with flush toilets and air conditioning. A nice mansion on the south shore of Pangea would be acceptable."

"For us, it could trigger war," said Dr. Cheetah. "We can hardly improve our reputation in the world by becoming a sanctuary for terrorists."

"We intend to be discreet," said Sunday. "The world doesn't even need to know we're there."

Dr. Cheetah tented his fingers together in front of his face. "If you were anyone else, this matter would not even be considered."

"But I'm not someone else. And, if it weren't for my father, you wouldn't be smart enough to have a country where we could try to seek sanctuary."

Dr. Cheetah nodded, but said nothing. Only the faintest shadow of his eyes could be seen through his veil. He looked lost in thought.

Pit Geek had gotten involved with Rex Monday only about ten years ago. Long before Monday had turned to building an army of meta-human terrorists, he'd spent several years building weapons to be used against his hated foe, Dr. Know. For much of that time, he'd succumbed to the dream of every evil super-genius and spent uncountable hours designing ray guns. Freeze rays, heat rays, shrink rays, disintegration beams . . . no sooner had he built one than he'd move on to perfecting the next.

One of his projects had been the evolution ray. He originally planned to build a devolution ray, something that would turn his enemies into gibbering ape-men. But when he encountered technical challenges with his regressive evolution ray, he decided to whip together a progressive evolution ray from the spare parts to see if he'd gain any insight to help him solve the puzzle.

The ray worked, at least on his chimpanzee test subjects. Over the course of a summer he tested his evolution ray on 2,000 chimps, making certain he'd solved the technical challenges.

Then Dr. Know unleashed Rail Blade upon the world. With her ferrokinesis, she destroyed Rex Monday's base in the Congo. In the aftermath, Dr. Know faced the ethical dilemma of what could be done with a hundred score talking chimps with average IQs of 170. They were no longer wild beasts; they couldn't simply be released back to the jungle. Nor were they merely hairy humans. They could never truly be integrated into the society of any existing country.

However, in a lucky bit of timing, Dr. Know had only months before found an engineering solution for the ecological disaster unfolding in the north Pacific gyre. In the 1980s, sailors began to report back that there were vast expanses of the Pacific filled with dense concentrations of floating plastics. Soda bottles, plastic bags, scraps of lawn furniture, and millions of miles of nylon rope and nets were congregating in an area the size of the continental United States. The sheer expanse of the mass was causing severe ecological imbalances as some microscopic life thrived in the mess, out-competing other microbes that had long been the base of the food chain.

Breaking the plastics down only created more surface area for the harmful microbes. So, Dr. Know decided on the opposite solution. He designed small solar powered skimmers to collect the plastic in the gyre and shepherd it to a central location. The garbage patch the size of the US was swiftly reduced to an artificial landmass not quite the size of New Zealand. Dr. Know anchored the new land to the ocean floor with long chains of repurposed plastic. Birds began nesting on the shores, with their waste forming the foundation of a nutrient rich soil. Many plant species took hold. Dr. Know had extensive plans to landscape the place, but, finding himself deciding the fate of a small army of super-apes, he decided to give the island to them to make of it what they wished. Thus was born the nation of Pangea.

After a long moment of silent contemplation, Dr. Cheetah shook his head. "I'm sorry," he said. "Pangea possesses all the resources necessary to become a thriving nation. We have a prime location between the world's two largest economies. We're a nation of researchers and engineers; our intellectual property laws are the fairest on the planet. Many corporations privately express interest in partnering with our businesses. Only naked prejudice holds us back. We dare not give you sanctuary."

"But—" said Sunday.

"My dear, there is nothing you can possibly say that would change my judgment."

Then his cell phone chirped.

"This meeting is over," said Dr. Cheetah, pulling out his phone.

"Come on, Sunny," said Pit, standing up. Sunday looked like Dr. Cheetah's words had sucked the life right out of her. He offered her his hand to help her rise.

They walked away as Dr. Cheetah began his conversation.

"The Covenant did what?" Dr. Cheetah shouted.

They turned back to him. The chimpanzee was standing up in his wheel chair, his body trembling.

Pit looked up at the nearest television. CNN News was showing a large white mansion on fire. It looked like a slightly scaled down version of the White House. Beneath it was the caption, "Pangean Embassy, Los Angeles."

The camera was focused on the news anchor, but switched back to a reporter on the scene. A very unhappy looking Servant was standing next to him. The sound was off, but closed captioning was on.

Reporter: "What prompted this attack on an embassy?"

Servant: "Department of Homeland Security intercepted an encrypted phone call into the embassy. We have a verified voiceprint—the call was made by Sundancer. Not all of the call was deciphered, but we did have firm information that Sundancer and Pit Geek were meeting with the Pangean Ambassador at this hour."

Reporter: Doesn't this violate international law, to attack the sovereign soil of an embassy?

Servant: It would also be a violation of international law for the Pangeans to meet with these fugitives, or withhold information on their whereabouts.

Reporter: But the raid didn't unfold as planned.

Servant: We arrived inside the Ambassadors office unannounced, but without taking hostile action. We did not find our targets, and intended to leave peacefully. Before we could vacate the premises, the Pangeans' robotic security forces initiated an unprovoked assault. We caused some damage in the course of defending ourselves, but I can assure you there were no human casualties."

Dr. Cheetah dropped his phone as these words appeared on the screen. "Three of my aides were killed!" he cried. "That monster!"

By this point, everyone in the food court was staring at Dr. Cheetah, and, by extension, Sunday and Pit. There had to be fifty cell phones pointed in their direction, snapping pictures.

Pit took Sunday by the hand and started to run back across the enclosed walkway.

"Ap and Skyrider weren't on the screen," said Sunday, breathing harder than she should have after running such a short distance. "Do you think they're back in action yet?"

"Maybe," he said.

"I can't believe that son of a bitch survived having a mountain fall on him," she grumbled.

The door to the elevator opened. A teenage boy practically walked into them. He was holding an iPad in his hand and a familiar voice was coming from the speakers.

"The robots had flamethrowers as well as guns," Ap said. "They caused the vast majority of the damage you're seeing on screen."

"Give me that," said Pit, snatching the iPad away from the kid half a second before the door closed. The sound of fists pounding on the door faded as the elevator began to rise.

The screen showed a web page. The banner read, "Ap Live." The screen was divided into two windows. In one window, Ap was smiling as he answered questions. In the other window, what looked like a blonde college-age girl in nerdy glasses was staring into a webcam.

"Ap," she said. "Code4U here! Such a thrill to finally meet you!"

"Hey Code, whatsup?"

"I was just wondering why you didn't use your foam mode to control the fire? Don't you feel it's important to save chimp life as well as human life?"

The elevator stopped at the third floor. Amazingly, the teenager they'd taken the iPad from had run up the flight of stairs next to the elevator and stood there panting as the door opened.

"Who are you, the Flash?" Pit asked.

The kid didn't answer as he grabbed at the iPad. Pit kept his grip on the device as Sunday kneed the kid in the groin and pushed him back out the door.

"I assure you I wanted to save all life. I controlled the fire as much as possible, but once it became clear that our targets weren't on site, and the confusion over who was attacking who died down, we were ordered to leave the grounds by the Pangeans themselves. Since we were no longer in hot pursuit, we had no choice but to comply. Rest assured, the Covenant will always respect the wishes of the appropriate authorities. Today, we just made a tough call in the face of two conflicting legal priorities."

The elevator doors wouldn't close because the iPad guy was too dumb to stay robbed. He kept throwing himself back into the gap just as the doors were about to close. Sunday kept pushing him out.

He ran at them again. With a sigh, Sunday held up her right hand and allowed it to burst into flame.

The kid froze in his tracks.

This time, the doors closed unimpeded.

Code4U asked, "So, if you're in L.A., do you have dinner plans? 'Cause I'm in school here and I'd love to meet you in person."

"Um," said Ap, looking flustered.

"I mean, not like a date," she interjected, suddenly sounding embarrassed. "I mean, you probably have a girlfriend."

"Well," said Ap, with an expression that was almost a grimace. "It's like this. I . . ."

He cupped his left hand to his ear. "I have reports the terrorists have been spotted. We've got to go!"

The signal in Ap's window blipped out, then just as quickly reappeared. The burning embassy was no longer the backdrop. Now, behind Ap, there were large concrete columns and row after row of cars.

"Oh shit," said Sunday.

Then, the elevator shot up like it was a rocket. The sudden acceleration knocked them both to the floor.

"Oh shit!" screamed Sunday. With a horrible jolt, the steel cage that carried them smashed through something above them.

Code4U vanished from the second window of Ap's webcast and was replaced by streaming video from an unknown source showing the elevator bursting out of the top floor of the garage. Skyrider was under the car, lifting it. Servant was on top of the car, kneeling. A pale yellow plasma flowed from his hands and coated the steel box he stood on.

"Close your eyes," said Sundancer, her hand flaring. "I can't cut loose without frying you, but let me get outside."

Pit closed his eyes, but could still see light dancing before him. There was a smell like the burner of an electric stove turned to its highest heat. Seconds passed. Then more seconds. Pit opened his eyes as the light faded.

"Power trouble?" he asked. "Need some help?" This wasn't the best location to help get her powers jump-started again, but he was at least willing to try.

"This metal isn't burning!" she snarled, rubbing her hand. "I can't go hotter without cooking you!"

On screen, Ap was crawling up the elevator shaft. The box was a tiny dot in the sky by the time he reached the top and turned his camera on it.

"We've got them!" he cried. "Skyrider is going to fly the elevator to a secure holding location, while Servant is reversing his time aura to maintain the integrity of the elevator. Basically, Sundancer can throw all the power she wants at it, but time is passing so slowly for the molecules of the box that it would take weeks before the damage appears!"

"Well now," said Pit. He handed Sunday the iPad, then smacked his lips. "This looks like a job for Pit Geek."

"Just do it," she said.

"I've been wanting to say that line for years," he said. Then he pressed his lips to the door and sucked.

The explosion that followed peeled the flesh right off his face.

The first murders were accidents. But in Tijuana twenty years later, I wasn't hurting anyone. I don't remember how I'd got my power under control, but I only ate what I wanted to by then. I don't even think I remembered those first guys I killed, but it's difficult to remember when you forgot to remember a memory.

Some punk gang-bangers threw me in a well in Tijuana. They'd point a spotlight down the hole. Faces I couldn't make out would lean over the well and watch as my handlers shot AK47s down the hole. "Zombie!" they'd scream, and laugh as I flailed around, not dying. "Zombie!"

There was a middle-aged man with no left ear who used to show up drunk in the middle of the night and pour gas on me, then toss in a burning newspaper. He wasn't charging people to watch, like the gang-bangers. He just liked to hear me scream.

I was down there for months. One day a rope got tossed down. Don't know who did it, or why. They didn't stick around. I couldn't have asked when I climbed out; I'd been shot in the head so many times I'd lost the capacity for speech. Took months to get it back.

Took hours to kill everyone in a five-block radius. Men, women, children. I didn't know who'd paid to see the zombie. I didn't care.

I wonder if the person who threw me the rope had any regrets.

I wonder if I killed them.

Burn Baby Burn

Chapter Eleven
Hollow

WHEN PIT HAD pressed his face to the elevator, it looked to Sunday like the whole box had warped and curved like a fun house mirror. There was a high-pitched whistle that caused her molars to vibrate. Then the metal walls had shattered into tiny fragments. Pit's face tore, his lips splitting in half a dozen places, the wound's racing up his face. When the windblast hit, the skin peeled back like a banana, leaving his skull staring at the vanished door with a look of wide-eyed surprise.

Skyrider's helmet slammed into Sunday's coccyx half a second later. Sunday had apparently been standing directly over her, and when the floor tore apart, collision had been inevitable. Sunday wound up sitting on Skyrider's shoulders, with the lower rim of the faceplate of the woman's helmet cutting into her pubic bone.

A huge, ugly naked man flashed past her, limbs flailing as he tumbled down, following Pit Geek's path toward the ground at least a mile below. If they were a mile up, he had thirty seconds before he hit. When she'd first learned to fly, she'd educated herself rather thoroughly on these things.

She tilted her head back, gazing at the sun, and released herself. Heat and light exploded from her. Before, Ap's foam had prevented her from really blasting Skyrider. Now, Skyrider took a dose of energy that should have reduced her to atoms. Instead, the two women were thrown apart by the energy burst. Sunday quickly regained control of her flight. Skyrider spiraled downward, trailing smoke. Her outer garments had been burned away, revealing a skin-tight mesh, like pantyhose woven from silver, covering the woman's body. Her helmet crumbled as she fell, but by now she was too far away for Sundancer to focus on her face. The woman had spiky red hair and, judging from the limpness of her limbs, the blast had left her unconscious.

Sundancer arced downward, blasting the air behind her to accelerate. She assumed Pit could survive having his face torn off, but wasn't as sure that he could shake off the damage that would be done if he hit the pavement after falling for a mile. She'd studied this subject. She'd seen pictures. The human body effectively turned into a water balloon.

Servant had now fallen past Pit Geek. He was once more dressed in white. He had his feet pointed downward, cutting his wind resistance. Why would he want to fall faster?

Sunday reached Pit a quarter mile above the ground and cooled her right hand so she could grab his collar. She felt like her arm would rip from her socket as she tried to slow his fall. She went into a dizzying spiral as the ground raced closer. As the landscape spun, she caught a glimpse of Servant hitting the pavement in the middle of the parking lot, feet first. Asphalt flew everywhere. Then the hero bounced back into the sky as if he'd had springs on his heels. He flashed toward Sunday and Pit. She screamed as she tried to pull out of her dive.

Servant drove his shoulder into the small of her back. She was certain her spine had snapped as her legs went numb. The impact tore Pit from her grasp. He was limp as a corpse as he fell.

As she tumbled through the air, she saw Servant fall as well. Apparently, while he could jump, he really couldn't fly. He landed on the pavement feet first, turned into a white blur that ran thirty feet to his right, held out his massive arms, and caught Skyrider like a football, hugging her to his chest, crouching to absorb the impact. The rescue flowed so smoothly Sunday couldn't help but grudgingly admire Servant's versatility.

Now only yards above the ground, pure instinct kicked in and Sunday flared to a higher brightness. The ground beneath her vaporized. Cars up and down the block suddenly exploded. The radiation pouring down from her skin acted like a giant pillow and her fall came to a gentle stop. She shot back into the sky, once more in control of her flight. While her lower spine felt like it had been hit with a sledgehammer, she could once more feel her legs. She looked down. Her survival action had filled the air below her with smoke and dust. She spun 360 degrees to find where Pit had landed.

Only, Pit hadn't landed. Instead, he was dangling in a net like the world's ugliest fish. The net, in turn, was hanging from the strangest aircraft she'd ever seen. Dr. Cheetah turned his face toward her and gave her a salute. His wheel chair had been transformed. The wheels had folded down perpendicular to the body of the chair and now whined as they spun like rotors, providing lift. The handles on the back of the chair had folded out to form a tail. Dr. Cheetah piloted the whole thing with a joystick held in his lower left foot.

He spun the heli-chair around and pressed a button. Two missiles shot out from beneath the vehicle. An instant later, Servant and Skyrider vanished in a small mushroom cloud.

Sunday flew closer to the Doctor. "Good shot!" she shouted.

Dr. Cheetah pointed a finger at his ear then made a few hand signals in sign language. Sunday didn't know ASL, but she gathered he was saying he couldn't hear her.

The mushroom cloud cleared. Servant was flat on the ground, face down. Skyrider was nowhere to be seen. Then Servant rose on his hands and knees, revealing Skyrider underneath him, looking unharmed by the blast.

Directly underneath Dr. Cheetah's chair, a brown balloon was floating up. Sunday squinted, unsure she was seeing what she was seeing. It looked like Ap dangling from the bottom of the balloon. And the balloon was made from the top of his scalp? She was fairly jaded when it came to physical abnormalities, having spent years in the company of a giant baby doll with a revolver for a head, but this . . . this was disturbing.

Dr. Cheetah scooted the heli-chair backward, away from Ap. He pressed another button and a second nylon net shot out from underneath the chair, trailing a steel cable. The well-aimed net wrapped itself around Ap's body, pinning his arms. Dr. Cheetah began to reel him in. Then Ap's head deflated with a farting noise and the net fell right through Ap's body as if it wasn't even there. Ap spread his limbs like a skydiver as he fell toward the ground at a tenth the speed a normal body would have fallen.

"Dr. Cheetah!" Sunday screamed, as Servant suddenly leapt for his chair. Fortunately, the chimp's reflexes were as superhuman as his intellect. He nudged his joystick to the left and Servant's grasping fingers closed on empty air as the heli-chair scooted away.

Dr. Cheetah pointed west. They weren't far from the ocean. He tilted his joystick forward and raced toward the sea. Sunday followed. She saw Pit struggling in the nylon netting that hung from the bottom of the heli-chair. She hoped he'd regain his wits enough to fish out the regeneration ray. Only, what if his powers didn't work if he no longer had lips? And just what had caused the explosion? Her father had said that Pit's mouth seemed to warp space. Servant had been warping time to keep the elevator intact. Had the competing warps both catastrophically failed?

They reached the beach. Sunday looked back over her shoulder, wanting the satisfaction of seeing smoke and flames pouring up from the mall area. But instead of satisfaction, she felt a chill as the white blur left by Servant's uniform dodged among cars on the crowded boulevard in hot pursuit. He dove into the waves and proved to be just as fast a swimmer as he was a runner. Sunday could definitely outrace him, but Dr. Cheetah's heli-chair struck her as relatively pokey. If he was pushing it to top speed, that speed was a hundred miles an hour. They were almost a mile up. From what she'd seen, Servant couldn't jump this high. But what did that matter if he simply hounded them until Dr. Cheetah was forced to land? The heli-chair didn't look as if it were designed for long distance travel.

A direct attack was useless. Servant's force fields had taken everything she'd thrown at him. But she had to discourage pursuit somehow. Maybe she could blind him? Could he see through steam?

Even better, could he swim through it?

Sunday raced out a mile in front of Servant, then dropped so that her feet nearly touched the water. She waited ten seconds. Then she let loose with the same level of heat she'd used to melt the West Virginia mountaintop. The water formed a bowl beneath her as she vaporized the ocean for a quarter mile in every direction. Servant shot out of the waves in front of her, his arms and legs flailing as he suddenly swam in empty air. He fell toward the muck below.

She shot toward the heavens as the ocean shuddered and uncountable gallons of water roared into the hole she'd left. Servant hit bottom. He raised up, shielding his eyes as he gazed at Sunday. Then the water crushed in on him, tidal waves hundreds of feet tall dropping down from every direction.

She lowered her intensity as she gave chase to Dr. Cheetah. She gasped. It suddenly felt as if a thousand ice-cold needles had been driven into every joint. She jerked erratically across the sky as her limbs began to tremble. It was the same weakness she'd felt back in West Virginia. What was wrong with her?

Clenching her fists, she drew on pure will power to bring her flight back into control before she hit the water. They were several miles off shore now. Geography wasn't her strong suit, but the closest shore of Pangea had to be at least fifteen hundred miles away. Could she make it that far? Could the heli-chair?

Then, as if she didn't have enough problems, a large dark shape began to rise through the water beneath her. It had the outline of a shark, but even great whites weren't this big. It looked to be at least two hundred feet long.

A gray fin knifed up from the water. The mega-shark kept rising, until its back was completely out of the sea. Waves churned around it as it slowed.

Dr. Cheetah piloted the heli-chair down toward the broad flat area behind the creature's head. He gingerly set Pit down, then deftly guided the heli-chair to a gentle landing a few yards away. A hatch suddenly lifted up from the shark's back and three chimps scurried forward. One slung Pit over his shoulder while the other two assisted Dr. Cheetah.

Sunday dropped onto the back of the shark.

"What's going on?" she asked as she let her flames flicker away.

Before anyone could answer, she fell, her body slamming onto the sharkskin. It felt like rubber stretched over steel. Her limbs shook uncontrollably as a million invisible dentist's drills dug into her bones. She vomited, unable to lift her head. Her thighs grew hot as her bladder emptied.

Dark spots danced before her eyes. The last thing she saw was a chimp's hand-like feet running toward her.

SHE OPENED HER EYES in a hospital room. She winced as the whiteness of her surroundings stabbed at her eyes. Turning her head, she saw an IV stand with a bag of red fluid and a bag of clear fluid.

The acute pain she'd felt when she'd landed had faded, leaving her with a diffuse, hollow ache that ran from her toes to her scalp.

Pit was sitting next to her. He was slumped over in his chair, his face pressed into the sheet on the edge of her bed. His fingers were draped over her left arm. He was drooling.

"Pit," she said.

His eyes cracked opened. He sat up, rubbing his face. Once more, he was clean-shaven.

"You used the regeneration ray?" she asked. Her voice sounded very faint.

He took her hand, clasping it in his grasp. "I was gonna try it on you, but Dr. Cheetah said that ain't a good idea."

She nodded. "I've felt funny ever since I used that thing." She sighed. "After it takes me apart, I'm not certain it's putting me back together right."

Pit shook his head. "The gun don't hurt me none. I'm probably to blame for your problems." There was a look of genuine remorse on his face.

"How are you to blame?"

"You'd been in hiding all those years," he said. "Not using your powers. Then I talked you into robbing all them banks. I wore you out."

"Maybe," she said, though she was almost certain that something was going on beyond mere exhaustion.

"Where are we?" she asked.

The door opened. Dr. Cheetah poked his head inside. "Am I interrupting?"

"Come on in, Doc," said Pit.

"I was just asking where we were," said Sunday.

"We're aboard the *Megalodon*," said Dr. Cheetah. "It's a prototype submarine that will form the foundation of our naval forces." Then his eyes flickered around the room. "Your more immediate surroundings, of course, are the medical ward of said vessel."

"I picked up on that, thanks," said Sunday. "Any theories as to why I need to be in here?"

"Some, yes," said Dr. Cheetah. He produced a large tablet computer from a drawer at the foot of the bed. It was bigger than an iPad, a little thinner, and instead of an Apple on the back it had a small yellow banana. He held it forward to reveal an ex-ray. Against the black and white bone, thousands of little green holes could be seen. Dr. Cheetah panned in and these proved to be computer generated circles highlighting tiny pockmarks in Sunday's bones. He handed the tablet to Sunday so she could look closer, but she really didn't understand what she was looking at.

"We've spent many years reviewing your father's data, and—"

"How?" Sunday asked.

"How?" Dr. Cheetah furrowed his brow. "We read them, mostly."

"No, I mean, how did you get the data? My father used to have a shadow network hidden through computers all over the world. I could tap into it from anywhere, until he disappeared. Then the network just vanished."

"Ah. Yes. That would be our fault."

"How so?"

Dr. Cheetah waddled around to the side of her bed on his short monkey legs to check her IVs. "We Pangeans worked closely with Dr. Knowbokov for several years to establish our new homeland. However, our true loyalties remained with Rex Monday. He had, after all, given us the gift of mind. Our agents stationed at the Knowbokov compound reported the death of both Dr. Know and Rex Monday. The two men had acted as if they were the gods of this world, but in the end, neither could survive a bullet to the head."

"So my father is dead," she said, softly.

"Such are the reports," said Dr. Cheetah. "Immediately following Monday's death, we Pangeans backed up all the data on his shadow network, then wiped all traces of it from the various servers that had hosted it. We didn't wish this information to fall into the hands of others. The advanced technological designs stored in his data bases provide the foundation of our current industries."

Pit was staring at Dr. Cheetah with a focus that made even Sunday a little uncomfortable.

"Is something wrong, Mr. Geek?" Dr. Cheetah asked.

"You can walk," said Pit. "I thought you needed a wheelchair."

"The chair was merely part of my disguise. If I'd walked, humans would have been instantly mindful of the differences in my gait, no matter what clothing I wore."

"Let's get back to my problem," said Sunday, staring at the tiny pits on her bones. "You said you have data on me?"

Dr. Cheetah nodded. "Since puberty, you've manifested the ability to generate tiny wormholes that channel solar material. It's an amazing ability. If we could somehow duplicate it mechanically, it would provide all of earth with limitless, abundant power."

"And you could make one hell of a bomb," said Pit.

"Yes. That." Dr. Cheetah looked satisfied with the state of the IVs and turned his gaze once more to the tablet that Sunday held. "The cells of your body that generate the wormholes originate within your bone marrow. From what I can glean from your father's notes, when you shut off your powers when you were younger, the wormholes collapsed in under a picosecond. While we need to run some tests to verify this, the pattern of damage to your bones suggests that, for the faintest fraction of a second, the spin of the wormholes is inverting before they vanish. Instead of material from the sun flowing out through you, material from you is flowing back into the sun. When you turn your powers off, you are effectively flushing blood, bone, and marrow down very tiny toilets. This is the cause of your current pain."

"The regeneration ray," she said. "Did it—"

"Possibly," said the chimp. "Mr. Geek informs me that your problems began after you'd used the gun on yourself. It's possible that your restored cellular structure has slight variances that are the source of your condition. But we can't rule out the possibility that this effect has always been present in your powers. It's not reflected in your father's data, but we have much more sensitive instruments than he had available ten years ago."

"My powers didn't hurt me ten years ago," she said.

"You were younger and more resilient," Dr. Cheetah pointed out. "And please note that the effects we're talking about here take place on scales far smaller than can easily be imagined. It may simply have taken a long time for the damage to accumulate to critical levels. You've never had the power to channel more than a very tiny percentage of the sun's total energy through your wormholes."

"What?" asked Pit Geek. "Like, one percent?"

"Like one billionth of one percent," said Dr. Cheetah. "If she could channel one percent, she would reduce the earth to cinders."

"As long as I keep my powers burning, I don't get hurt?" she asked. "In theory, I would never have any pain as long as I don't shut the wormholes down?"

"In theory," said Dr. Cheetah. "Though I suspect such a

course would have a deleterious effect upon the quality of your life."

"Can you fix her, Doc?" asked Pit. "Could we just use the regeneration ray?"

"That ray caused my problem," Sunday said.

"The good news is, the body is capable of regenerating lost tissue," said Dr. Cheetah. "With some rest and good nutritional practices, your pain should abate and your strength should come back. For most of the time you have left, you won't always feel as bad as you do now."

"Most of the . . ." Sunday's voice trailed off.

"I'm sorry," said Dr. Cheetah, shaking his head. "But you've exposed your body to massive doses of radiation for nearly a decade. Your cells are growing back. Unfortunately, some are growing unchecked. We've tried to map the location of all the tumors in your bones. Some may be benign. Some are almost certainly malignant. I fear they are innumerable."

"Cancer?" asked Pit.

Cheetah nodded. "Once we're in Pangea, we can discuss treatment options. In the meantime, I would refrain from using your powers. L.A. is still cleaning up from the tidal wave you triggered. I worry if you use your powers in such spectacular a fashion again, you might not survive the aftermath."

Sunday turned her face away from Pit. The last thing she wanted to hear at this moment was some stupid speech about running toward the Grim Reaper.

"You can't let her die, Doc," said Pit, squeezing her hand. "I love her."

And so he did. And though she couldn't imagine ever saying the words, she loved him. At the moment she learned she would die, she finally felt as if she had something to live for. She shut her eyes and managed not to break down.

And then,
for a little while,
we were happy.

Chapter Twelve
Monkeys and Robots Make Everything Better

THEY ARRIVED IN PANGEA in the middle of the night. Sunday was feeling better after a blood transfusion and two days of rest. The sub had run deep, cut off from radio, and Pit had expected that when it finally surfaced they would be surrounded by battle ships and superhumans waiting to take them back to justice.

Instead, they surfaced in an utterly changed world. Pit didn't have much interest in politics, but as Sunday read news on the internet, she tried to explain things so he'd understand. The US had faced worldwide condemnation for the embassy attack. China took the incident as evidence that the US was planning a full-scale invasion of Pangea. A decade ago, the place had been an embarrassing morass of soggy trash that no country wanted to deal with. Now, Pangea was turning into an island paradise in an enviable location. China had seen the pattern before. The US would claim that a country was harboring terrorists, then use this as an excuse to conquer the country. The US disavowed any attempt at turning itself into a colonizing power, yet countries around the world were falling like dominoes as the US invaded and installed friendly governments willing to give US corporations generous contracts.

The Chinese had finally had enough. If the US used force against Pangea in the absence of clear and incontrovertible evidence, China vowed to retaliate. The threat was diplomatically vague. Perhaps it meant military action, though America had enough to fear if China implemented economic sanctions.

"Does that mean the Covenant can't chase us?" Pit asked. "Does it mean we'll be left alone?"

"I think it just might," she said.

Once on shore, Dr. Cheetah drove them along a highway that followed the sea. It was a full moon and the water gleamed in the light. The car was a convertible, and the night air was rich with the fragrance of flowers. Later, Pit would learn that ninety percent of the automobiles on the island were convertibles, since chimps took delight in the sensation of wind rushing through their fur. But, on this evening, all he knew was that he was in the back seat of an open car with the woman he loved pressed against him and the sea and the sky stretching on forever.

They were provided with a seaside villa that had been built as a vacation home for the notorious African dictator Zesty Manbuto. Alas, Zesty and every member of his immediate family, and a frightening number of uncles, aunts, cousins, second cousins, and complete strangers who'd borne a mild family resemblance had recently been executed in the aftermath of revolution. The Pangean villa had been built with money channeled through illegal bank accounts. There was no legal documentation proving it belonged to anyone. It had been built to accommodate humans, so the chimps didn't want it. (As Pit had discovered during his time on the sub, chimps built their sinks and counters at the level of his kneecaps, and their toilets barely stood higher than his ankles.) Dr. Cheetah assured them that, for a fraction of their stolen wealth, they could call the place home.

It was nearly morning when they got to the mansion. Pit thought it looked like a museum with its marble floors and columns. The master bedroom had a bed that looked built to accommodate orgies.

"Zesty had large appetites," said Dr. Cheetah. Then he'd opened the door to the balcony and they'd followed him out. A long lawn landscaped in palm trees and spiky bushes stretched down to a beach white as snow. Despite the tropical vegetation, the air was a bit nippy.

The moon had vanished. The sun lit the water aflame as it rose to the east. Sunday squeezed Pit's hand.

"We'll take it," she said.

Pit had been unaware they were being given a choice, but he played along. "Sure," he said. "It's perfect."

After Dr. Cheetah left, he and Sunday tried out the bed. He was cautious, worried about hurting her. They kissed gently for a long time, but he made no motion to take things further. He knew she still wasn't feeling as well as she should.

Finally, in frustration, she grabbed his hand and clamped it onto her breast.

"I'm just dying," she said. "I'm not dead."

And then he'd given up on gentleness and caution, determined to test her physical limits. An hour later he was out of breath and too sore to crawl away as she pulled him to her once more.

"I might need the regeneration ray," he'd said as she grabbed hold of parts of his anatomy that were ready to surrender.

"Or you might just need some extra encouragement," she'd said, sliding beneath the sheets.

They wound up sleeping until sunset. They awoke drenched with sweat. They got sweatier for a time. Then they went down to the climate-controlled swimming pool to cool off. They floated around on water lounges while tiny swimming robot butlers brought them piña coladas. Sunday finished her fifth drink and went completely limp in her lounge. Pit thought she might have gone to sleep.

Then she whispered, "I think there's something wrong with me."

"Naw," he said.

"I'm so . . . happy," she whispered.

"Oh." He scratched his chin. "I ain't sure I'd call that wrong."

"Shouldn't I be scared?" she asked. "They tell me I'm dying and it's like a weight off my shoulders. War is over. I fought the world and the world won. And now I'm just so . . . so . . ."

"Drunk?" he offered.

"At peace," she said. "Maybe it's endorphins."

"You ain't gonna die," said Pit. "Dr. Cheetah said he'd have ways to treat you."

"We're all gonna die," she said. "No one gets out alive! It's like your motto, Mr. Positive."

"Well, sure. But there's no need to be in a hurry."

"I'm not in a hurry. It's just . . . I don't know."

"Yeah?"

"I've killed a lot of people. A lot."

"You keep count?" he asked.

"No," she said, then laughed. "It didn't matter to me." She shook her head. "Those rednecks in the bar. All those cops. Who knows how many people I took out back in L.A. when I went nova to stop my fall. I didn't see their faces. They didn't see mine. I had nothing against them. I was just some force of nature, mowing them down, without asking if they were ready, without asking if they'd had time to do everything they wanted to do, without caring if they were in love, or in pain. I pushed death upon them with utter indifference."

She motioned for the bar-bot to make her another drink. She let her hand drop back into the water while she waited.

"And now," she whispered. "Now it's my turn. Whether I'm ready or not has nothing at all to do with it."

"I ain't ready," said Pit. "I ain't ready for you to go."

With a soft whir of underwater jets, the pool-bot brought her next drink out to her.

"Damn, these are good," she said, after sucking down half the glass. Then she rubbed her temple and squinched her eyes together. "Ow!"

"What's wrong?" asked Pit, jumping up from his lounge and bobbing toward her in the chest deep water.

"Brain freeze!" she said. "I drank too fast."

"Oh," said Pit. "That's the worst."

She sighed. "Not even by a long shot."

Pit climbed back into his floating lounge. Sensors directed jets to stabilize the chair as he positioned himself. "This is pretty fancy stuff," he said. He leaned back and looked up at the stars. "Yeah, the good life."

Sunday sighed as she, too, leaned back. "Monkeys and robots make everything better."

A FEW DAYS LATER, they met with Dr. Cheetah. They'd spoken on the phone a few times, but he told Sunday he had news he needed to deliver face to face. He arrived with a second chimp. In L.A., the embassy chimps had worn clothes to make their human hosts more at ease. On Pangea, all the chimps went naked. This meant, unfortunately, that when the two chimps arrived, Pit couldn't tell the two of them apart. He hoped he'd pick up on some clue as to which was Dr. Cheetah so he wouldn't look like a jerk to the ape who'd saved their lives.

"How are you feeling today?" one chimp asked as he approached Sunday.

"Not bad," she said. "Borderline normal."

"The pain has lessened?"

"Some," she said. "I still have stiffness, and sometimes I get these little needles of pain digging around in my shins. But I had a hangover the other day that put things in perspective. I don't want to be a wimp about this. The pain is manageable."

"Excellent," said Dr. Cheetah. Then, he turned to the second chimp. "Allow me to introduce my superior, Dr. Trog."

"Trog?" asked Pit. "Ain't that some kind of monster?"

"I think not," said Dr. Trog. "The scientific name for chimpanzees is pan troglodytes. I found the shortened form more aesthetically pleasing. I'm surprised you wouldn't recognize the origins of my name, given that humans have provided the labels for every living thing. I fear I must question the quality of your education."

Pit furrowed his brow. Was he being insulted by a monkey? Then he grinned. Maybe the ape had him figured out. "I ain't sure I had no education."

"Indeed," said Dr. Trog. He turned to Sunday. "And you are the meta-human whose own powers have damaged her?"

"Guilty as charged," she said.

Dr. Trog said, "I've reviewed your scans and blood work thoroughly. I've come to present you with options to deal with your bone cancer. I fear none are very good."

"Hit me," said Sunday.

"Ordinarily, bone cancer is treated with drugs and radiation. Unfortunately, your tumors don't possess the genetic markers that would respond to the most effective drugs. Radiation is normally used to target a few localized tumors. You have tumors throughout your body. My colleague may have used the unfortunate phrasing 'every bone in your body' during an earlier conversation. This is nowhere near the truth."

"Oh?" Sunday asked.

"The human body has 206 bones. You have tumors in 93 bones, fewer than half."

"Oh," said Sunday.

"Of course, this is still too many to make surgery an option. If the bones were confined to a limb, we could consider amputation. Since you have tumors in most vertebrae and in several ribs, this is hardly a practical solution."

"Of course," said Sunday.

"We could attempt to treat your tumors with a broad spectrum of chemotherapy not dependent on your genetic makeup. However, due to the widespread nature of your disease, the doses would be massive. It's a case where the treatment could shorten your life more than simply allowing the disease to run its course."

Sunday nodded. "If it runs its course, how long do I have?"

Dr. Trog shook his head. "I can't say. There are no previous cases that quite match your condition. I can't point to any given tumor in your body and say, 'Here. This is the one that will kill you.' With your meta-human physiology, I can't rule out the possibility of spontaneous remission. However, given the extent to which the disease has progressed in the relatively short time since you first used the regeneration ray, my informed opinion is that you likely have only weeks left to live."

"Will I be in pain?"

"Pain can be treated," said Dr. Trog.

"I guess we'll just let the disease go where it goes," she said.

"I can't take that," said Pit.

"It's not your call," said Sunday.

"We can just keep using the regeneration ray on you," said Pit. "Rebuild you every morning. You ain't gotta die!"

Dr. Trog shook his head. "I fear she's lost mass with each exposure to the ray. You will only increase her agony with such a course of treatment."

"I'm done with the ray," she said.

"This isn't fair!" Pit shouted, throwing up his hands. "Why is the ray working on me and killing you?"

"My understanding is that you possess enhanced recuperative powers," said Dr. Trog. "The ray may indeed harm you, but your natural biology mitigates the effect."

"Then put my blood in her," said Pit.

"Excuse me?" said the chimp.

"Put my blood in her. Won't that heal her?"

"You know nothing of medical science, my good man. Your blood types are incompatible."

"How do you know that?" asked Sunday.

Dr. Trog said, "It was among the biological information we recovered from the ray."

"When did you recover information from the regeneration ray?" asked Sunday. "Have you even seen it?"

"No," said Dr. Trog. "Of course I haven't recovered any information from the regeneration ray. What are you speaking of?"

"You just said—"

Dr. Trog held up his hairy hand. "My apologies. I misspoke. We were talking of the ray and the word was simply in my mind. I meant to say, of course, the biological data we gathered from your father's records."

"Did those records show why I can heal?" asked Pit.

"Not that I can recall," said the doctor.

"Then find out. Put me in a machine. Study my blood. You monkeys are supposed to be geniuses! I'm a damn puzzle. Solve me!"

There were several seconds of silence as the two chimps gazed at one another.

"We have nothing to lose," said Dr. Cheetah.

"It would be cruel to inflict false hope," said Dr. Trog.

"Think of what we might learn!" said Dr. Cheetah. "Whether we cure Sunday is barely relevant. If we could market a drug that safely healed any wound suffered by humans, think of the fortunes to be made. Think of the prestige that would be due our country."

Dr. Trog turned from his colleague, waving his hand. "I care nothing for prestige in human eyes. And to me, a drug that cured humans and had no effect on our own species would be a drug I would flush down the toilet. Humans number billions while we number in the mere thousands. Why should we use our genius to save them?"

"Until we understand his powers, we can't know that a treatment based on them would only affect humans. We could be saving the lives of chimps as well."

"Do as you wish," said Dr. Trog. "I need fresh air. I shall wait for you in the car."

Sunday furrowed her brow as Dr. Trog closed the door behind him. "Are you sure he's doing all he can for me?"

Dr. Cheetah nodded. "He's a professional. I fear we've simply exposed a political rift among us Pangeans. Like humans, we chimps have our factions. I represent a political party who wishes to promote trade with humans. I would like to see humans view our island as a desirable location for tourism. The truth is, our nation needs to establish itself as an economic power if we're to thrive. On the other hand, Dr. Trog represents a faction of chimps who feel that Pangea should become completely independent from humanity."

"Then he's probably not fond of seeing us here," said Sunday.

"No," said Dr. Cheetah. "And Pit's use of the slur 'monkey' cannot possibly have endeared you to him. But, again, Trog's a professional. I can assure you his personal feelings do not in anyway influence his ability to provide you with the best possible medical care."

Sunday nodded.

Pit stared out the window and watched Dr. Trog climb into the convertible. He'd be keeping an eye on this one. If Sunday wasn't taken care of, well . . . out of all the crazy stuff he'd put in his mouth, he'd never swallowed a monkey. There was a first for everything.

AP WAS IN THE COMMAND CENTER working with Nathan to update the firmware of his belt when Servant came in and walked up to Simpson, who was sitting at the controls of the space machine, reading comic books. When none of the Covenant was out on a mission, Simpson really didn't have that much to do.

The command center was cavernous, half a football field long and several stories high, so from the other side of the room Ap couldn't hear what Servant said as he handed Simpson a sheet of paper.

But he did hear when Simpson turned, started tapping in the provided coordinates, then said, loudly, "Wait a second. These aren't the coordinates for Seattle . . . this is Pangea!"

Servant cringed as all eyes turned toward him.

Servant tried to shush Simpson, but Simpson was a nerd straight out of central casting who'd never really learned to control the tone of his voice. He sounded a bit like Jerry Lewis as the Nutty Professor when he said, "You almost got me! Ha, that's a good one, Mr. Servant!"

"Oh lord," muttered Nathan, rolling his eyes. "What a moron."

Technically, everyone in the room except for Ap and Servant was a certified genius, but Ap got the gist of Nathan's sentiment. Nathan snapped the side panel of Ap's belt closed. "There," he said. "Your belt had a vulnerability that could have been exploited by a Trojan application hidden in one of your powers."

"How likely is that, though?" asked Ap. "You guys run everything through the simulator."

"Do we?" asked Nathan. "Because I found a couple of vision powers in the buffer that hadn't gone through the normal review channels."

"Oh," said Ap. "Right. Those were from trusted sources."

"An anonymous hacker in a chat room is not a trusted source."

"I've . . . uh . . . I've met Code4U. Sort of."

"And I don't want to know what the application Swinging Pipe does."

"No, you don't," said Ap. "But I'll uninstall it at once. The vision stuff as well. I don't know what I was thinking."

"Good," said Nathan. "Then we're done."

Across the room, Servant and Simpson were done as well. Simpson was grinning, laughing at a joke only he was getting. Servant exited the room with a furtive glance over his shoulder.

Ap used his belt to trigger his Shadow mode. He hadn't yet found an invisibility program that actually worked, but Shadow got him to 95% transparency. With Servant stewing in his failure to get to Pangea, Ap had little trouble slipping past him by hugging the wall and dashing around the corner. He leaned up against a support column, casually crossing his arms.

Servant turned the corner and paused when he saw Ap.

"That went well," said Ap.

"Shut up," said Servant.

"You were going to provoke an international incident," said Ap.

"It wouldn't be an incident if no one found their bodies," said Servant.

"Whoa," said Ap. "No more Mister Nice Guy."

"Right now there are two known mass murderers living like royalty in a luxury mansion, according to our satellites. You can just sleep at night knowing that we could solve this problem for good?"

"By my scorecard, they've kicked our butts twice," said Ap. "Why would this time be any different?"

"Because last time we swept in pretending to be heroes, intent on capturing them. This time, I'm going in as a rogue agent. No one is authorizing my mission. The president can condemn my actions and launch a manhunt for me. I won't even resist if they find me. I'd gladly spend the rest of my life in jail to bring these two monsters to justice."

Ap shook his head. He'd expected to playfully tease Servant. He hadn't expected quite this level of seething anger.

"Look," said Ap. "I'm not happy about this development. But orders are, unless Pit Geek and Sundancer show up on American soil, we can't touch them."

"There are things more important than orders."

"Yeah. Like the law."

"There's man's law. And then there's God's law."

"I'm not a Biblical scholar, but isn't that eye-for-an-eye stuff Old Testament? If you're really a Christian, shouldn't you be a turn-the-other-cheek kind of guy?"

"Don't question my faith."

"Fine. Then I'll question your brains. You aren't Ogre any more. You're trying to be better than that. We're all trying to be better than that. You saw the line of toys that Mrs. Knowbokov is putting into Wal-Mart. Kid's all around the country are going to be playing with a little Servant doll this Christmas! How cool is that?"

Servant sighed. "Pretty cool I guess. Did they make the doll of you where the head blows up like a balloon?"

"Yep. And a Shadow Ap made of clear plastic. Another Ap where you can swap out the feet and hands for various bio weapons. Honestly if anything cooler has ever happened to me, I can't think of it. And yet, somehow, I still can't get any dates."

"Code4U came on pretty strong."

"You know the fundamental problem with that equation."

"Really want to try that Swinging Pipe mode, huh?"

Ap's cheeks burned. "You heard that?"

"Everyone heard it weeks ago. Nathan told Sarah and Sarah told everybody."

"Great," sighed Ap.

"Everyone knew your secret any way."

"Code4U didn't."

"Maybe she was borne without gaydar."

Ap crossed his arms. "Maybe it shouldn't be a secret. I mean, I've left the closet door pretty wide open, but I haven't actually stepped out of it. Maybe it's time."

"Whatever," said Servant. "I hope, one day, you'll come around to the truth and let me introduce you to some people who can cure you."

"Why am I talking you out of going to Pangea?" Ap asked, scratching his head. "Wouldn't my life be better if you were a wanted fugitive?"

"I'm already a wanted fugitive," said Servant.

"Right."

Servant exhaled slowly, his shoulders sagging. He shook his head. "But there aren't any dolls made of that guy. I guess . . . for now, I'll play by the rules."

"It would be a shame to bring down the value of our collectables," said Ap.

Servant nodded.

Ap chuckled. "Maybe we could put out a Sundancer doll. Trick her into coming back to the US to demand her royalties."

Servant didn't laugh, but the joke triggered a cascade of thoughts in Ap's head.

"Light bulb mode!" said Ap. Suddenly, a glowing egg bulged up from the top of his head.

"What the hell is that?" asked Servant.

"I just had an idea!" said Ap. "We wouldn't break any laws at all if we could drag Pit and Sunday back into US waters."

"You've got an idea how to do that?"

"Maybe," said Ap. "Exactly how strong are you again?"

Unless I find more bullets or a
different gun, I've killed my last goat.
A chicken, every now and then, can be
pegged with a rock and stunned. Goats
just run away.
Two bullets left.
One for her.
One for me.

Chapter Thirteen
The Secret Origin of Pit Geek

THE CT SCAN showed his head was full of shrapnel. No surprise.

What was surprising was when Pit tapped on the image of his brain and said, "Let's take it out."

Sunday wasn't sure she understood him. "Take what out? Your brain?"

"All the metal in my head," said Pit. "I've been getting shot in the head on a regular basis for damn near sixty years. It ain't killed me. But it's messed up my memory something fierce. So, we cut it out, and I remember who I am."

Dr. Cheetah scoffed loudly. "Cutting through the required tissue would leave you a vegetable. I might as well run your brains through a sieve."

"If that would get the metal out, let's try it," said Pit.

"Pit, I appreciate you want to help me, but I can't let you cripple yourself," said Sunday.

"I'll get better," said Pit. "I always heal."

"Brain tissue isn't like skin or bone," said Dr. Cheetah. "It doesn't regenerate."

"Mine might."

"My oath reads, 'First, do no harm.'"

"Mine reads, 'You gotta scramble some eggs if you want an omelet.'"

"Your brains are already scrambled if you think this is a smart idea," said Sunday.

"Yeah," Pit said, tapping his finger on the dark black shards that littered the scan. "This picture shows how scrambled they are. All I'm asking is that we unscramble them."

"It's amazing you're alive," Dr. Cheetah said, as he turned the image back and forth on the computer. "But it's also possible that these images are corrupted. Look." He rolled his mouse back and forth, twisting the image of Pit's brain from side to side. He tapped some of the black shapes. "See? This shard is plainly visible from the front. But it vanishes when we turn the image thirty degrees. Then, when we turn another thirty degrees, it's back! I'm getting a similar effect on a dozen fragments."

"Aw, just go in and poke around," said Pit Geek. "You don't need no fancy gadgets. Just a good knife and maybe a sifter."

Dr. Cheetah shook his head. "If you were anyone else, I'd never do this."

"You're not doing it to him!" said Sunday.

Dr. Cheetah sighed. "I understand your reservations. But Pit is now my patient as well. He plainly has serious, chronic injuries that greatly reduce his quality of life, in the form of his fractured memories. His curious biology does give him a better than average chance of surviving this procedure."

"You're both crazy," said Sunday.

Dr. Cheetah shrugged. "Why don't you both sleep on it? If you wish to have the surgery, I can perform it tomorrow."

"You'd perform the surgery yourself?" asked Sunday. "I thought you were more of a general practitioner."

"My dear, I'm a surgeon, an architect, a computer programmer, an attorney, and a novelist. Also, until recently, a diplomat. Pangeans are few in number. We must wear many hats."

"I haven't seen any of you wearing hats," said Pit.

"It's a human idiom," said the doctor. "I confess, our language is riddled with them. Until recently, all literature was human literature. Perhaps after a century of chimpanzee language, humans will begin to adopt our idioms."

"Like what?"

"For instance, when we face difficulties in reaching a goal, we say, 'the fattest ants are always lip biters.'"

"Okay," said Sunday. "I'm not sure it will catch on, but I get it."

"The dung you fling at your enemy sticks beneath your own nails."

Sunday nodded. "Makes sense. I can almost imagine it catching on."

"Even the dominant female must endure a slick anus."

She stared at him.

"It means—"

She held up her hand to stop him. "I honestly don't want to know."

THERE WERE OTHER THINGS she didn't want to know, but found out anyway. They'd driven to Goodall, the capital city of Pangea, since this was where the hospital was located. While it was the largest city on the island, it was still small enough to walk everywhere. From one end of the town to the other wasn't even a mile. The town didn't even have stoplights.

The hotel had been built with several floors to accommodate humans. The place was stuffy and filled with mosquitoes. Pangeans didn't like air conditioning; it robbed enclosed spaces of any smell except that of the air conditioner. Dr. Cheetah explained that this would be like decorating a human room with a single unvarying shade of beige. So, windows were left open, and bugs came in, including a spider in the bathtub big enough to have its own zip code. Pit Geek chivalrously devoured the arachnid so that Sunday could take a shower.

In the evening, they went out into the streets to see the nightlife. Every third business was a grooming parlor where rows of female chimps wearing white gloves fussed over their chimp clientele, laboring to pick away all the fleas and ticks that had accumulated during the day. They passed a bar where a chimp band called the Hoot Pants was getting the small crowd to wave their hands in the air as they hooted and panted. These all seemed to be harmless imitations of human businesses until they passed an open-air restaurant that resembled a sushi bar. Only, instead of a glass case full of dead fish, there was wall of small cages holding live tiny primates, small monkeys and lemurs no bigger than pug dogs. A group of male chimps were passing a tablet computer around with schematics for some kind of engine. Most chimps spoke in sign language, but these three had the vibrating implants that gave them voices. They were practicing their English by talking through their marketing plans for a zero emission airplane. They were drinking bright red juice from coconut bowls. At least, Sunday hoped it was juice.

But her hopes were dashed when the largest chimp pointed to one of the cages. The chimp stationed at the cage had a leather apron around his neck, with the pockets stuffed with knives and cleavers. He pulled a screaming lemur from a cage and carried to the chimp's table. They shoved their computer into a briefcase as the butcher chimp slammed the still wiggling animal down on the table hard enough to stun it. Then he pulled a cleaver with a blade nearly two feet long and eight inches wide and swung it with a grunt. The lemur was perfectly bisected, falling open like an especially gory anatomy book. The chef then produced a razor sharp white ceramic butcher knife. His hands were practically a blur as he cut the lemur's organs free of their connective tissue, then stepped back. The three chimp's fought one another to get the two halves of the brain. Two of the chimps hooted as they chewed up their pink prize. Then, one said in buzzing English with a perfectly bland Midwestern accent, "If you don't get the brain, you gotta suck the kidney."

The chimp who'd had no brain to eat pulled the left kidney out of the bisected primate and popped the purple organ into his mouth. He didn't look happy. He crossed his arms, and sulked.

THE NEXT MORNING, Sunday was covered in welts from mosquitoes. She appreciated the love of smells, especially as a gentle breeze blew floral scents through the room, but didn't understand why window screens hadn't caught on.

She pulled her knees to her chest and stared at Pit, who was still sleeping.

Then he snorted, and looked at her with one eye half open.

"Good morning," he said.

"I don't suppose you've forgotten what happened yesterday?" she asked.

"Probably some of it," he said.

"How about. . . ?"

"I want the surgery," he said.

"Fine." She slid next to him, pressing her body close, drinking in his warmth and his odor. "You better not come out of this a vegetable. I love you, but I'm not changing your diapers."

"Yeah, you would," he said.

"Yeah," she sighed. "I would."

SUNDAY CHEWED HER NAILS as she sat in the surgical waiting room. The surgery lasted well into the afternoon. A young female chimp passed through the room every hour, offering her bottled water. Sunday wasn't thirsty.

Which was ironic, since Sunday was certain she was in hell. In the years she'd worked for Rex Monday, he'd engaged in constant mind games designed to leave her contemptuous of other people's lives. She'd been an easy target. She'd hated every man her mother had brought into the house and despised her mother for not being a stronger woman. Monday had convinced Sunday that her innate superiority to ordinary humans had already begun to manifest at a young age. It was natural that Sunday felt no empathy for others, because there were no others who were her equal.

Now that she was twenty-five, she could see how easy it had been for a fifteen-year-old to fall for a father telling her she was better than everyone else. He'd been able to take the baseline alienation and rebellion present in any teen and puff it up into full-blown psychopathic isolation, where Sunday had stood heroically alone as an inheritor of truth and power in a world populated by dull, nameless shadows she would never care to know.

How easy it had been.

How easy it had been to kill.

She thought about all cops she'd burned, and all the wives and mothers who'd waited in rooms just like this for word of whether their loved ones would live or die.

If Pit did die . . .

If . . .

If Pit did die, she would turn herself in to the authorities. She knew she'd be executed. And maybe, in some small way, this would bring some tiny comfort to all those widows and orphans she'd created.

The female chimp came into the room. Instead of offering water, she said, "Dr. Cheetah would like to see you."

SHE WAS LED to a brightly lit room where Dr. Cheetah was staring at an array of peanut sized bits of black metal laid out on a blue plastic tray.

"Is he . . . ?" she asked.

"The surgery encountered difficulties," Dr. Cheetah said, sadly. He shook his head. "His brain tissue . . . we underestimated his regenerative abilities. His brain tissue was healing nearly as quickly as we could pull out metal."

"Then is he . . . is he . . . ?"

"I'm sorry," said Dr. Cheetah. "I didn't mean to create an air of suspense. The surgery was, perhaps, a failure. But Pit has survived. We won't know the state of his mind until he wakes, but he seems strong. He was . . . we gave him enough gas to tranquilize an elephant yet he kept coming to. We had to halt the surgery before we'd removed all the shrapnel."

"But you took out all this?"

"We took out far more than this," said Dr. Cheetah. "I have another tray filled with bullet fragments, shrapnel consistent with a hand grenade, the broken tip of a knife blade, the shaft of a bar dart, and three nails."

"And what are these?"

"These are eleven of the twelve anomalous fragments we saw on the CT scan. The ones that vanished at certain angles."

"Okay. But what are they?"

"My dear, since you are the person most familiar with Mr.

Geek, I was hoping you could tell us."

She tried to pick one up. It dropped from her fingers instantly. The fragments looked like lumps of hard coal, but this one had been as yielding and wobbly as a water balloon, and surprisingly heavy. She picked up another one, cupping it in her palm. She rolled it forward with her finger and it vanished, though she could still feel the weight in her hand.

"They turn invisible?"

"At certain angles," said Dr. Cheetah. "But more than invisible. From certain angles, they can't even be touched."

Which seemed to be the case now. Her fingers couldn't touch the unseen weight on her palm. She shook her hand, and a black lump flew off and landed on the floor.

"Be careful, please," said Dr. Cheetah, reaching for the fragment with his long arm. "We can't afford to lose what seems to be a very exotic form of matter."

"Forget losing it," she said. "You say Pit still has a piece of this in his brain?"

"One large piece, roughly the size of his thumb. Perhaps some smaller fragments as well. The scan has many mysterious shadows that measure no more than a few millimeters."

"Fragments?" she said. "Do you think these were once part of something larger? Do they fit together?"

Before Dr. Cheetah could answer, she picked up two bits that looked like inky Cheetos. She jammed the curved bits together. For some reason, they wouldn't touch.

"What do you think—" Before she completed her question the two halves flowed together into a ring roughly the size and shape of a mini-donut. It lifted from her palm and floated at the level of her eyes. Then, the donut swelled to the size of a bagel as the fragments on the tray vanished one by one. The whole process took only seconds.

Then the lights went out.

PIT GASPED as he woke in darkness. His entire skull was on fire. Sounds, pictures, smells, textures, and tastes flashed in his mind too quickly to grasp.

He knew who he was. He knew how he'd stopped being a man and turned into a monster.

1956. FRANK MACEY stared into the mirror at a face he didn't recognize. His thick black curls had gone gray and stringy. His square, ruggedly handsome face had begun to sag. His stubble was flecked with gray. He hadn't bathed in almost a week.

What was the point? He hauled garbage for a living. He was up before dawn every day dumping metal cans full of rot and filth into a truck that smelled like evil, a scent that rose from a black sludge caked into every crevice and cranny of the vehicle, a smell that had gotten into the pores of his skin and would never wash away.

He'd been famous once.

"Stick-em-up," he said to the mirror, pointing a finger at himself.

He hadn't come out west to play bad guys. Everyone back home had told him that with his looks and talent, he should be the leading man in films. His prophesied success had nearly come true. He'd been hired on the first audition he'd gone to. He'd tried out for the role of the sheriff. The director had said his nose was too big.

"You Jewish?" the director had asked.

"No," Frank had answered.

"You got kind of a look about you," the director said. "Something mean about your eyes. I can see you as a bad guy. Say, 'stick-em-up,' for me."

Frank did a quick draw with his finger and barked, "Stick-em-up!"

"Not half bad," the director said.

Frank had been on screen for the first two minutes of the film. He'd come out from behind some bushes when a stagecoach had stopped to move a fallen tree from the dusty trail. He'd fired his gun once overhead as a warning, then yelled out his line. The leading lady had screamed and Dallas Smith, Texas Ranger, had shot the pistol from his hand. Then he'd jumped from the stagecoach and knocked Frank out with a punch to the jaw.

Audiences loved it. Something about Frank's face made it a face they enjoyed seeing take a punch. He'd gone on to open other films, robbing banks and saloons and trains and riverboats and even a church. He'd gotten more lines. In some films, he'd been able to tack on, "This is a robbery!" In others, he'd shouted, "Dallas Smith!" in surprise and despair when the ranger had popped up from behind some random bit of scenery and shot the gun from his hand.

The job had paid good wages, but Frank never stopped wanting to play the leading man. But anytime he'd try out for another movie, he'd be told that audiences didn't want to see the Stick-Em-Up Kid get the girl.

Frank hadn't been able to get the girls in real life, either. His on-screen persona was of a guy who couldn't take a punch. A punk. A loser. And ladies wanted heroes.

Except, some ladies only wanted money. He'd had to get good and drunk the first time he screwed up his courage to pay a whore. When the Dallas Smith franchise came to a tragic end, Frank ran out of money for both booze and whores, so he chose the booze.

Now it had been ten years since he'd last been in a movie. Ten years since he'd come to Hollywood wanting to be a hero, only to learn he had a bad-man's face.

He got dressed in the coveralls he wore to work. They were stained and stiff with gunk. In his pocket was a Colt 45. He drew it and pointed at the mirror. He delivered his line.

Then he shot his reflection in the face.

FRANK WAS STARTING his garbage route and finishing a bottle of scotch when he'd turned the truck west and started driving toward Vegas. It was four in the morning. He'd be over the state line long before anyone noticed him missing. In Vegas, people walked around with cash in their pockets. Frank would enjoy some cash in his pocket.

Unlike the movies, his gun was filled with real bullets. No one was going to be punching him inthe jaw after he delivered his lines.

And then, just minutes before dawn, on a trackless stretch of highway with not a single car or building for ten miles in any direction, he ran into. . .

Actually, he didn't know what he hit. A thing. He'd run into some thing. It looked almost like an elephant, if you removed the legs and just allowed the beast to levitate two feet off the ground, balanced on a pencil-thin shaft of glowing red light. It had no trunk or eyes or ears, just a mouth as wide as the bumper of Frank's garbage truck. It was dark purple, drifting right down the white dotted line that divided the highway. Frank had been doing seventy, the top speed the truck could handle.

He went through the windshield when his truck plowed into the creature. He should have been killed, but the floating beast was blubbery. Sinking into its body was like sinking into a bathtub filled with lard and covered with a blanket.

And then the beast tore apart, and the wheel of his truck bounced past him, and garbage was thrown all over the dark desert.

He slid along the asphalt, his coveralls shredding. When he finally stopped, he almost felt cheated to still be alive. When he sat up, the beast's sickly green blood was bubbling away, evaporating with a smell like ammonia, vanishing into thin air.

All that was left after the accident was scattered garbage, lumps of blubbery meat, and a truck so pulverized Frank couldn't even spot the engine block.

"What the hell?" Frank asked.

His words were answered by a humming sound that released three pulses that matched the cadence of his words.

"Someone there?" he asked.

Again, three pulses of sound.

Then a black donut appeared in front of his face.

It hummed three times.

Frank reached for his gun.

The donut floated forward and placed itself against his forehead. It was warm and soft, and suddenly there was a voice in his head not his own.

"My apologies," the unseen voice said. "Do not be alarm—"
Frank twisted his arm to place the barrel of the gun against
the metal ring that touched him. The bullet was aimed straight
at his own forehead. It would kill him if it passed through the
mystery object.

He felt as if this would be the best possible outcome.

THE DONUT FLOATED into Pit's recovery room. Dr. Cheetah
and Sunday followed close behind it. Sunday had lit up a single
finger to provide light.

"If you use your powers, it might kill you," said Pit.

"It's just a finger," said Sunday. "I'll be okay unless I really
light up again."

Pit's focus turned once more back to the floating black donut.

"What the hell is that thing?" he asked.

"I am Eleven," the donut answered.

Man, woman, and chimp all stared at it, wide-eyed.

"I have learned your language in the years you have hosted
me," said Eleven. "I apologize if my previous attempts to
communicate caused you discomfort."

"You . . . you were inside me?" Pit asked. "In my head?"

"Yes," said Eleven. "Part of me continues to reside within
you. I thank you all for freeing enough of my form to allow me
to reintegrate at least partially."

"What are you?" Pit asked again.

"I am Eleven," the thing answered.

"Is that a name or an age?" asked Sunday.

"It equates most closely with the human concept of a name,"
said Eleven. "My age would be difficult to convey in your
language."

"You apparently know numbers," said Sunday. "How tough
can it be?"

"I am a seven dimensional explorative construct," said Eleven.
"Time moves backwards in my sixth dimension, and
orthogonally in my fifth and seventh dimension. If I were to
calculate my age using your constrictive enumerative systems,

my age would be expressed as a negative number."

"Dr. Coco will be most anxious to speak to you," said Dr. Cheetah. "He recently proposed a unified field theory operative in seven dimensions."

"This conversation cannot occur," said Eleven. "I'm forbidden to interfere with the cultural development of the inhabitants of planets I study."

"You damn well interfered with me!" said Pit.

"This was never my intention," said Eleven. "You drove your vehicle into my vehicle. You met my attempt at telepathic communication with an act of violence. The kinetic energy of your weapon shattered my form and lodged my components within the matrix of your nervous system."

"Vehicle?" said Pit. "You were driving a damn purple elephant down a dark highway! I wouldn't have hit you if you'd been in something with headlights."

"The bioship glowed quite strongly in infrared," said Eleven. "I was not aware of your species' limited ocular range."

"Why have you stayed inside him all these years and never said anything?" asked Sunday.

Suddenly all the lights came back on. She let her finger fade back to its normal state. Her face didn't show any pain.

"My sentience could not emerge while I was fractured," said Eleven. "I could not heal myself without damaging my new host's brain even further. Of my ninety-three restrictions, the first is that I shall do no harm."

"But you did me all kind's of harm!" said Pit. "You stole my memories. You made me a damn zombie monster!"

"Even in my non-sentient state, my core programming was designed to maintain a bioship. Any damage you have accrued over the years has been repaired. My repair mechanisms strove to keep you in the exact state I found you in. With minor improvements to your fueling systems, of course."

"My fuel . . . you're the reason I can eat anything? And don't go to the bathroom?"

"Your evolved fuel systems were wasteful and inefficient. You would never build sufficient power for interstellar travel through primitive chemical digestion. All of your world seems woefully underpowered. The rather minimal energy I pulled from the environment to rebuild myself was sufficient to damage this structure's electrical systems. You're the most energy efficient creature on this planet, Frank Macey. I've fueled all of your biological needs for over five decades with only the mass of the three humans you devoured when you first opened the warp portal. The excess mass you've consumed is being kept in extra-spatial stasis until such time as it is sufficient to power your travel through interstellar space."

Pit didn't really know what to say to this.

Sunday, however, cut to the question that should have been on his mind: "Now that you're not in him anymore, does he still have his powers?"

"I am still inside him. I must maintain my host's systems as long as he hosts fragments of my physical shell."

Pit reached into his mouth and drew out the regeneration ray. "You're in luck, Space Donut. This baby has a 'remove foreign material' setting."

Sunday surprised Pit by jumping forward and snatching away the ray. "No one is removing anything," she said.

"Th—sk—ha," said Eleven.

"What was that?" asked Pit.

"My apologies. I was merely stating that it would be wasteful to remove me at this point. Given that my subroutines have already altered your body to serve as my vessel, I'd like to remain within you until such time as I complete my study mission. Plus, there is an attractive symmetry in transforming the body of the being who ruined my last bioship into my new bioship. I apologize that I could not express this on my previous attempt. The device Sunday is holding is emitting radio waves that interfered with the voice channels I had selected."

"What do you mean, it's emitting radio waves?" asked Sunday.

"I'm unsure how to make my statement any clearer," said Eleven.

"What's it transmitting?" she asked.

"Real time data of our conversation, plus physiological data on the bearer's body temperature, heart rate, and the ph levels present in sweat."

Sunday turned to Dr. Cheetah, her voice sparking with anger. "You knew about this, didn't you?"

"I swear I knew of no such thing."

Sunday pressed her lips tightly together.

"Dr. Trog," she said.

"Of course," said Dr. Cheetah.

"Will one of y'all tell me what you're talking about?" asked Pit.

Sunday started yanking IVs out of Pit's arm.

"Ow!" Pit screamed as the needles tore from his veins.

"You'll survive, you baby. I need you dressed in one minute." She turned to Dr. Cheetah. "Does Trog have an office in this hospital?"

"Of course," said the chimp. "He should be there now."

"Lead us," she said. "We can't let him get away."

Pit got out of bed, feeling a little woozy from the massive amounts of gas they'd pumped into his lungs to keep him under. "Who's getting away? What are we in such a hurry about?"

"My father is dead!" said Sunday, throwing open the doors of a white cabinet. She said, "Yes!" as she found his clothes. She tossed them to him. "So if Rex Monday didn't send us a regeneration ray, who did?"

"Dr. Trog? Why?"

Sunday shook her head like she was frustrated by how stupid Pit was being. "He said he'd been studying our biological data! That machine tore us down to our DNA and put us back together. For all I know, he's trying to give himself our powers!"

"Since your powers are killing you, this seems unlikely," said Dr. Cheetah. "Still, I would like to discover the truth."

Pit yanked on his pants and threw off his hospital gown. He grabbed his shirt and headed for the door. "We'll come back later for my boots."

Then the floor shifted sideways beneath him and he slammed

face first into the wall. He tried to balance himself, but the floor continued to jump and tremble. The IV poles toppled and everything attached to the walls fell off and landed with a crash.

"Earthquake!" Pit yelled.

"Impossible!" shouted Dr. Cheetah, as he clung to the edge of the swaying bed. "We have no earth to quake! Pangea sits atop a fused mass of floating plastic. We cannot be affected by seismic action!"

"Then how the hell do you explain this?" shouted Sunday.

WHAT NO ONE IN PANGEA could know was that, far below, on the seabed, the anchor chains had all been severed. The central chain, the strongest, was now in the grip of a large man in white tights with a red S on his chest. Servant strained as he pulled the chain northward. He was determined to keep his schedule. In two hours, the northern tip of Pangea would be within 200 miles of the southernmost Aleutian Island, and thus in the territorial waters of the United States. In two hours, Pit Geek and Sundancer would finally face justice.

I learned to type back in 1943. I'd taken my motorcycle out to the high desert to stay with an old buddy of mine who'd been a stunt man until he lost his arm. The two of us spent all our nights drinking. By day, I'd sit in the attic, writing a screenplay, tapping it out with two fingers. I'd make a mistake and tear the paper out and toss it in the can. I cursed a lot that summer.

THE STICK-EM-UP KID GETS THE GIRL.

The Stick-Em-Up Kid never had a real name in the movies, but in the script it was Pete Green. He'd come west to mine for gold but fell in with a bad crowd. Took to robbing stagecoaches, but he never killed nobody.

The gang leader was named Mick Silver. Silver spotted a young girl named Susie Hart inside the stagecoach and dragged her out, telling her she was going to cook and clean for the gang. But Pete tells Silver to leave her alone. They wind up fighting. Pete kills Silver, and has to flee. Susie rides away with the handsome and mysterious outlaw, since she doesn't want to be left alone in the desert.

They flee into Indian territory. After overcoming a series of obstacles (a swollen river, a pit of snakes), they meet a good Indian named Black Wolf. He warns Pete that a band of bad Indians is headed to the Gold Hart Ranch to kill everyone and steal the cattle. We discover that Susie's father owns the

ranch. Pete rides his faithful steed
Lightning to save the day. He kills all
the bad Indians and saves Susie's father
from scalping.

As a reward, he's allowed to ask Susie's
hand in marriage.

They ride into the sunset, living
happily ever after.

In the movies, one good deed erases a
lifetime of crimes. No one demands
justice for old sins.

I sometimes stare at the revolver,
thinking about the remaining bullets.
Thinking about old sins. Thinking about
how sometimes, in the real world, nobody
gets the girl.

Chapter Fourteen
A Terrible Actor

PIT DIDN'T BOTHER to button his shirt as they ran toward the elevator banks. Unfortunately, the shaking of the building had disabled the elevators.

"Are there stairs?" Pit asked.

"Our legs aren't really built for stairs," Cheetah said, opening a door a few yards away from the elevator. Inside was a series of parallel ladders. "We're more comfortable climbing," he said, leaping onto the bars. He descended, shouting "Dr. Trog has an office on the first floor. We're on the sixth floor. Hurry!"

Sunday leaned into the ladder bank, staring at the long drop to the first floor. "It would be quicker if I flew," she said.

"You know what the Doctor said."

"Don't nag me," she grumbled. Then she grabbed the rungs and started to go down. "I don't like feeling helpless."

"You ain't helpless," said Pit, grabbing the rungs. "You're still my better half. Hell, I'd still be on that bed talking to a space donut if you hadn't figured this all out."

"Where did Eleven go?"

"Damned if I know," said Pit. "Just sort of disappeared once all the shaking started."

When they arrived at the lobby, the place was in chaos. Chimps on stretchers were screeching loudly as hairy orderlies raced them out to the streets.

Dr. Cheetah was halfway across the lobby, running on all fours. He spun and called to them, "Hurry! The whole building may collapse upon us if this continues much longer. This structure was built to withstand typhoons, but the designers never planned for an earthquake. They simply can't happen here!"

Pit and Sunday ran, following the doctor deeper into the building, weaving through a stream of chimps heading in the opposite direction.

They followed Dr. Cheetah around a corner and found him shaking the handle of an office door.

"It's locked," he cried.

"I'm on it," said Pit. Then, even though he was barefoot, he ran at the door and put his full weight into a kick. The door splintered at the lock and swung open.

"Ow, ow, ow," Pit said, hopping. It felt like he'd cracked every bone south of his knee.

"Why didn't you use your powers?" Sunday asked.

"Aw, this way was more cowboy," Pit said with a grin.

"It was rather manly," she said approvingly.

Except for the fact that the desk was only two feet tall, the office looked like it could have belonged to a used car salesman, just a modest box of a room barely big enough for the three of them.

"This isn't a very fancy office for your top oncologist," said Sunday.

"We spend very little time in our offices," said Dr. Cheetah. His voice was nearly drowned out as the building groaned.

"That was ominous," said Sunday.

"We should leave the premises," said Dr. Cheetah. "The value of interrogating my colleague no longer exceeds the value of the risk."

"You go on," said Sunday. "We'll keep searching."

"But where will you even begin?" he asked.

"I'm thinking this secret door is a good place to start," she said, moving behind the desk.

Pit squinted. The lights were flickering, but Sunday might be onto something. The pastel green drywall behind the desk was cracked in a rectangle four feet tall and three feet wide. It looked like a panel that had fit perfectly flush until the twisting of the building had set if slightly ajar in the concealed frame.

Sunday pushed on it. When it didn't open, she leaned back

and kicked it. The door bounced back after the blow. She pulled it open and revealed a shaft with a ladder heading down. She crouched and hopped on. Pit followed, looking back. Dr. Cheetah stood in the doorway.

"The danger . . ." he murmured.

"You got no reason to get yourself killed," said Pit. "Get out of here."

Dr. Cheetah hung his head shamefully as he slinked back through the door.

The shaft was dark, lit only by the flickering light from the room above. The air in the shaft was cool and dank, smelling of damp concrete. The light grew dimmer and dimmer as they descended.

"I've found the bottom," Sunday announced.

Pit stopped. Her voice was so close, he was worried he might accidentally step on her.

"There's a door," she said. "Steel. We're not kicking this one down."

"Step aside," he said. "I can—"

"I'm not a cripple," she said. There was a sudden flash. Pit squeezed his eyes shut from the painful intensity. There was a *hiss*, followed by sharp, sour metallic smoke. Pit coughed and peeked downward. Sunday's right hand was glowing as she cut around the lock of the steel door. With a clatter, the handle fell out on the other side. Sunday pushed the door open. Pit dropped down.

The light around Sunday's hand faded. She frowned as she looked around the room. With her other hand, she rubbed her wrist.

"Are you hurt?" he asked.

"It's just all this ladder climbing and door kicking," she said. "Flying all these years has made me a little soft."

The room beyond reminded Pit of a parking garage, a vast space filled with pillars sandwiched between two slabs of concrete. Only, instead of cars, the room was packed with row after row of video game consoles and what looked to be at least a hundred refrigerators. If they were refrigerators. They were taller than normal, and seemed to be made entirely of dark glass. In the dim light, Pit couldn't make out the contents.

"The good news is, when the hospital collapses down on us, we won't feel any pain," said Sunday, eying the concrete slap above them.

However, Pit noted that the shaking and vibrations had calmed down considerably. Whatever force had set the building in motion seemed to be dying off. Either that, or the building above ground just shook more than the building below ground.

Sunday jumped as a noise came from the doorway to the ladder. Pit stepped in front of her, ready for whatever came out of the door.

It was Dr. Cheetah. "Sorry if I startled you," the chimp said, softly. "I was halfway outside when I changed my mind."

"Why'd you come back?" asked Sunday.

"When I represented Pangea as a diplomat, I had to monitor human media for what was said about our nation. It galled me to hear radio talk show hosts say that chimps could never display traits such as love, or honor, or courage, since these were purely the reserve of humans. As I was running from danger while you were pressing on in search of truth, these words were like burrs digging into my pride. I can't live with myself if I think that two mere humans have displayed greater bravery than I have."

"What if it's just greater stupidity?" asked Sunday.

Dr. Cheetah shrugged. "Let's move forward," he said.

They walked toward the nearest refrigerator with Dr. Cheetah in the lead. Suddenly, a row of green lights lit up on the ceiling in front of him. He swung forward in his four limbed gate. With a barely perceptible *hiss*, the front half of his body vanished in a display of bubbling lights. His belly fell to the ground leaving his rear end sticking up. Bright red blood poured out of him. Where it flowed forward, it turned into bright sparks and vanished. A line beyond which nothing could pass was clearly demarked.

Pit looked around. They were now standing inside of a ten-foot square marked by the green ceiling lights.

"How regrettable," said a voice to their left. Dr. Trog stood there with his hands behind his back, just on the other side of the green line. Unlike when they'd seen him last, he was wearing clothes. He wore what looked like a lead apron, the sort x-ray technicians might wear. And, he sported a wide black belt, similar to the one Ap had worn. He was gazing at the remains of Dr. Cheetah with a look of genuine sorrow. He sighed. "I suppose it was a bit fantastic of me to think I could accomplish this without the death of at least a few chimpanzees. And, if someone had to die, he was a worthy candidate. Pangea will be better off with one less human sympathizer."

"What did you do to him?" Sunday growled, letting her right hand flare up.

"It's unwise to threaten me, human," said Dr. Trog. "You'll lose that hand if you aren't careful. From the data I've gathered, the degradation of your physical structure accelerates with each use of your powers. Every time the wormholes damage your cells, they produce further mutant cells that generate defective wormholes."

"I'll take my chances," said Sunday.

"As you wish," said Dr. Trog, gazing up at the green square above them. "The lights on the ceiling are scanners for a teleportation beam. At least, the portion of the teleportation beam that tears matter apart. Alas, I have not installed the sensors needed to capture the data to restore my colleague. These beams are purely for destruction, meant to finish off unwelcome visitors."

Dr. Trog turned away, waddling toward a computer monitor and keyboard hooked into the networked game systems. "Curiously, I didn't design it to serve as a cage, and yet it seems as if it will serve that function perfectly."

"You made the regeneration ray, didn't you?" Sunday asked.

Pit took this as a cue. He reached into his mouth and produced the weapon once more.

"Of course I made the ray," said the chimp as he turned the monitor on. "But I wouldn't waste time training it on poor

Cheetah. His brain is gone. You could build a new body based on his DNA, but it would be a soulless, mindless copy."

"Why did you build this ray?" asked Sunday. "Was this an elaborate plot to kill me? What had I possibly done to harm you?"

Trog bared his teeth and hooted. "You flatter yourself to think I gave even a moment's thought to your fate. No, my interest in teleportation technology long predates you. I was aware that Rex Monday had once designed and tested a teleportation belt that proved more effective at tearing matter apart than it did in putting it back together. I coveted the technology. The small size of Pangea's population makes us vulnerable. But imagine how feared we'd be if the robots we employ for our defense were armed with disintegration beams!"

"So when you downloaded my father's data, you learned how to duplicate the technology."

"Even better!" said Trog, sounding delighted. "I had some data, true, and had made significant breakthroughs. I have no doubt that, in five years, I would have perfected the device. But then, to my astonishment, the original source code and schematics for the belt were posted on the internet!" He patted the belt he wore. "I've adopted an online persona of a young human female named Code4U and have been corresponding with the clueless Johnny Appleton to perfect the technology. I wrote his preferred Restore Mode code. It was a simple matter to transfer the technology to the gun you bear."

The chimp began to type with both his hands and feet. He kept talking. "Among your father's data, I found the dates and locations he was to use to contact you. I had quite a bit of information about your abilities from your father's notes, but craved further data. The possibility of weaponizing your wormhole generation was too tempting to ignore. The regeneration ray has recorded your genetic make up in detail and transmitted it to me. Now, you will be pleased to know, your physical form is effectively immortal. I need merely provide the raw materials in the form of a dead pig and my teleportation beam can build a carbon copy of you. A soulless, mindless copy, to be certain. But also a copy in full possession of your powers."

He glanced at Pit Geek. "Your mate, alas, was not as interesting. Whatever the source of his curious consumption and regenerative abilities may be, it does not seem to spring from his DNA."

Pit looked down at the concrete floor. It wasn't sparking. The disintegration beam was apparently calibrated to stop at this point. Could he eat a tunnel out of here?

Sunday asked. "So you can duplicate me. But my duplicates would have the same flaws that I have now. Their powers would kill them."

"True," said Trog. "Fortunately, they will only need to use them once."

With a click, lights inside the glass refrigerators lit up all at once. In every direction, they faced the horror of Sunday's nude, decapitated body, the head replaced by a small bank of webcams.

"I now command my own legion of Burn Babies!"

"Baby Burn," Sunday corrected him.

Trog paid her no mind. "I told myself I was building these purely for deterrence, but in truth, I always knew the day would come when I would unleash these on the earth's largest human cities." He tapped a few more buttons. "When these have accomplished their mission, Pangea will be the dominant world power! It shall be humans who live as animals in the forest!"

"I've never had the power to blow up a whole city," said Sunday. "You'll kill some people, sure, but then the armies of the world will strike back! You think a hundred headless copies of me are stronger than even a single nuke dropped on this place?"

"Most definitely. You've never unleashed your full power because your fears hold you back. My army has no such fears." With a tap of the button, robotic arms moved inside the containers and brought a syringe to the arm of each duplicate. With a jab, dark blue fluid flowed into the bodies."

"This is pure adrenaline," said Trog. "It will prime their cells for the fullest release of power. The cities of the earth shall be reduced to ashes!"

"Don't do this!" screamed Sunday. "The humans haven't attacked you. They've done nothing to deserve destruction!"

"Have you not felt the ground shaking?" asked Trog. "We're currently under attack. The Covenant member called Servant seems to be dragging us into US waters. The navy of the United States no doubt prepares to fend off our incursion even now. The truth of how our nation wound up moving across the open sea will almost certainly never be reported by human media."

"The Covenant doesn't want war with Pangea," said Sunday. "They want us! You can stop all this destruction simply by turning us over to them!"

"She's right," said Pit, his shoulders sagging. "It's us they want. We should have known we couldn't just run away."

"I assume this is a trick of some sort," said Trog. "The two of you have never shown the least bit of remorse for your crimes." He pressed a button. The glass doors slid open. "But, if it was a sincere offer it's too late. Perhaps you've doomed mankind by coming to Pangea. If this is so—" he looked at them with a twinkle in his eye "—I'll see that statues are erected in your honor."

The women throughout the basement began to glow. Waves of heat washed across the cement floor. In unison, they all began to march out of a steel door."

Trog stood up from the terminal and came to the edge of the green line. "Now I face the question of your disposal. I doubt you will voluntarily walk into the disintegration beam."

"Probably not," said Pit.

"And the second I leave to deal with Servant, you'll simply chew through the floor and escape," said Trog. "This would not be optimal."

"Aw, we ain't going nowhere," said Pit. "What do we care if you blow up the world? We're terrorists! Good riddance, I say."

"Has anyone ever told you that you are a terrible actor?"

Pit grimaced. Being a terrible actor had been the origin of every problem he'd had since 1938.

"Fortunately for me," said Trog, tapping a few buttons on his belt. "The grid array is mobile."

More of Dr. Cheetah's body vanished as the green lines on the ceiling closed in on one another.

Sunday turned to Pit. "Just one last time to do this, I guess." She wrapped her arms around his neck and kissed him.

Had to punch a new hole in my belt today. Just used a nail I found stuck in a two by four. I was skinny when I got here, but I'm now four belt-hole's thinner.

Almost completely bald. When I got here, I still had some dark hair in my beard, but now it's all gone white. I found a little round mirror on a stand, the kind you use for shaving. I look like someone's grandfather.

Spend most of my days sleeping.

Haven't eaten in a long time.

Funny, given that I'm surrounded by meat. Hundreds of severed human hands, some arms, a few feet, over a dozen heads. Still look as fresh as the day they got here.

I've collected them as I found them. One body, I pieced back together, like the world's grossest jigsaw puzzle. If memory serves, he was a lawyer from Kansas City.

Some people say we taste like chicken.

I don't guess I'll find out.

I might be a man-eater, but I ain't no cannibal.

Chapter Fifteen
BOOM BOOM BOOM

SUNDAY'S KISS LASTED barely a second. She pulled her lips from his mouth and pressed them to Pit's ears. "Close your eyes and duck," she whispered.

Pit ducked, covering his head, as Sunday pointed her hands straight up. Her fingers almost brushed the low ceiling.

The green beam reached the tips of Pit's knees as he squatted, his hands over his head. The fabric of his jeans vaporized as the advancing light reached him.

There was a *whoosh* and heat washed over him, singeing his hair. There was a sound like every kernel of popcorn in the world firing off in the space of a second. Flakes and fragments of concrete rained down onto him. The green light fizzled out as it cut a raw hole in his right kneecap the size of a quarter.

He stood up. Sunday was on fire from the tits up.

He said, his voice cracking, "You'll—"

"Hush," she said. "It only hurts when I turn my powers off. That's never going to happen."

Dr. Trog looked unflustered by Sunday's destruction of his disintegration grid. He calmly reached into a pouch on his belt and pulled out a gun the size of a derringer that looked like a miniature version of the regeneration ray. A red targeting light cut through all the dust in the air to land on Sunday's left breast. Pit shoved Sunday and jumped toward the chimp as Trog pulled the trigger. The beam took off most of his right ear and a chunk of his shoulder before he opened his mouth and swallowed the ape's hand, gun and all, to the mid point of his forearm. With his remaining arm Dr. Trog punched Pit in the cheek. Pit was knocked to the ground, stars in front of his eyes.

He spat out a molar as he tried to rise. Then he fell once more, his head still spinning. The chimp punched like he had a horseshoe hidden in his glove, if he'd been wearing a glove.

Fortunately, the ape didn't press his attack. Instead, he ran with inhuman speed, shouting, "Regeneration Mode!" as he veered suddenly to hide behind a concrete pillar. A ball of glowing white plasma hit the ground where he'd just stood, sizzling away, leaving a black scorch mark.

Even though she'd missed, Sunday's splattering plasma must have caught Dr. Trog at least a little, since the chimp gasped in pain as the smell of burnt fur polluted the air.

"Foam Mode!" the chimp screeched from behind the pillar.

Then, Dr. Trog whipped back around the column, the shaving cream like substance bubbling from his skin. He vomited a torrent of the goop at Sunday, forcefully enough that she was knocked from her feet like she'd been hit with a water hose.

The chimp leapt upon her and thrust his long canine teeth toward her throat. She twisted at the last possible second and he sank his teeth into the meat of her shoulder rather than into her jugular vein.

Sunday screamed, blowing the foam that covered her lips into the air in a spray of white bubbles. Pit rose to his hands and knees, blood trickling from his mouth. He reached for the chimp in a motion that was half lunge, half fall. He grabbed the ape's foamy right ankle.

An inhuman growl tore from Pit's throat as he summoned every bit of strength he had left to yank the ape off of Sunday. Fortunately, the foam provided lubrication, helping slide the super-intelligent chimp off. Dr. Trog rolled to his back and opened his foaming jaws, pink with Sunday's blood, inhaling to shout another command. Pit shoved the monkey's foot toward his jaws, and took the ape's leg off all the way up to the hip. Blood spurted from the severed limb as the ape screamed. Pit decided to add insult to the injury by delivering a sold punch to the ape's testicles.

The doctor arched his back and opened his jaws. He looked like he was screaming, but no sound came out. Pit dragged himself closer to the ape, sucked in, and the ape's hairy belly vanished as a tornado of entrails and organs spiraled down Pit's throat. Blood and bile and things Pit didn't want to think about flecked his cheeks.

He closed his mouth. The stupid ape was now gone from the rib cage down. Everything that should have been inside the hollow of his ribs had vanished. Pit sat up, wiping his face on his shirt.

His back grew hot as Sunday baked off the foam that had smothered her. He looked back, squinting, and found her staggering to her feet, her hand clamped over her injured shoulder.

"Just sit still," he said. "You're hurt. One of them monkey doctors upstairs can stitch you up."

"Give me the disintegration pistol," she said.

"What—"

"You just ate it!" she screamed. "I don't have time to argue! Give me the damn gun!"

Pit reached in and grabbed the gun, with the black leathery hand still attached.

Sunday's whole body was now glowing, save for her right hand, which was a dark spot against her radiance. She reached for the gun. Her hand was thin and wrinkled. Blood oozed from around her nail beds.

"Your hand—" he whispered.

"Will you just shut the fuck up?" she cried as she snatched the gun away. "I've got to stop an army of cyborg Sundancers from destroying the world!" She ran toward the door her duplicates had left through. "You start eating computers! Something down here must be guiding them!"

She jumped into the air and flew through the door, leaving behind only a tornado of sparks.

SUNDAY BURST from the tunnel she'd followed for half a mile to find herself in bright sunshine. She'd completely overestimated how much time had passed; she thought by now the sun would have set.

Spinning around, she found the moon in the sky and realized it was night. The false day was being created from the hundred duplicates of herself who stood at attention on a low hilltop off to her right. The headless women looked like some cryptic modern sculpture as they stood aligned in ten perfect rows of ten, each precisely one arm's length away from each other. They were pumping out enough heat that the hilltop beneath them had fused into black glass.

Sunday didn't know what they were waiting for. She didn't care. She suspected that no amount of heat and radiation she could throw at them would have any effect. Her own powers had never even made her sweat, though she was sweating now. Her heart was beating like she'd run up the tunnel rather than flown. Her fight or flight instinct had kicked in at full power.

So she did both, flashing toward the grid of bodies, firing the disintegration pistol almost blindly. Bodies began to topple as she swept the beam across the cyborg army. In seconds, she'd killed or seriously maimed over half. Could things really be this easy?

Then, the remaining bodies lifted their arms to her, and suddenly there was nothing in the world but fire. Sunday felt as if she was suffocating as the combined blasts of the assembled drones tore the molecules of air surrounding her into a slurry of elemental particles. She raced upwards, out of the blast zone, gasping as she reached breathable air. She looked down at the army and pointed the ray gun. When she squeezed the trigger, it was like squeezing clay that oozed between her fingers. The barrel of the gun drooped like a spent penis. Whatever its melting point had been, the drone attack had gone over that line.

She looked down at the remaining drones. They had stopped targeting her and now stretched their arms out stiffly to their sides. The dust and dirt flew up in a ring around them as fire shot out from their palms and feet, thrusting them heavenward like rockets. They lifted slowly at first, but accelerated so swiftly that they reached Sunday, hovering a quarter mile above them, in only a second. She shook her hand to clear it of the molten gun, then clenched her fists, braced for their attack.

Only, they weren't attacking her. They flashed past without even seeming to be aware of her. One passed less than a yard away and on pure instinct Sunday kicked it in the gut. Her stomach tightened from the impact; she'd somehow expected the guts to be hard, filled with robotics. Instead, it was warm and yielding, disturbingly . . . human. But, human or machine, the fortunate effect of the kick was that it knocked the drone off its trajectory, causing it to crash into a sister drone that rose only an arms length away. That drone spun out, and in a game of aerial dominoes, three more drones were knocked off balance by the veering bodies. As the naked women bounced off one another, green lights on the cameras atop their heads turned red. The affected drones went into tailspins as their robotic navigation systems lost control. They raced down to messy endings on the ground below, but Sunday had no time to waste watching them. She pushed herself higher, in pursuit of the surviving drones. She didn't pause to count, but there were still close to thirty.

Then, BOOM BOOM BOOM! Sunday was hit in the chest by a shockwave as the drones above her accelerated past the speed of sound. Now it was her tail in a spin. The ground raced toward her with sickening speed. But, she clenched her teeth and took control of her fall, leveling off a few feet above the ground, leaving a trail of burning earth behind her as she raced toward the chimp city of Goodall. She blazed down the main street, setting convertibles aflame, then whipped down the side street where the lemur sushi bar had been situated. She was doing 200 miles an hour when she neared the restaurant, crowded with dozens of chimps having dinner. The chef in his leather apron had his arm raised over his head, the cleaver gleaming with reflected light. She grabbed his apron and his arm as she sped past him. Unleashing a blast, she ripped the monkey's torso apart, leaving her holding a hand holding a cleaver, which she pried loose. She had the apron draped across her arm. She turned toward the sky as she fished the white ceramic carving knife free.

Years of experience had taught her how well certain materials held up to heat. The cleaver would warp and turn to putty at a paltry 2500 degrees Fahrenheit, but the ceramic knife could take twice that heat, maybe even three times as much depending on its specific makeup.

The drones were spread out in the sky in a straight line, just little dots of light. How could she ever catch them? She'd never been able to go past the speed of sound. Or had she just never had the courage to go past the speed of sound? Those were copies of her up there. Anything they could do, she could do.

With the knife in her hottest hand and the cleaver in the hand she'd cooled to carry the gun, she inhaled deeply, feeling tightness building in the pit of her stomach. If she flew that fast, the wind would peel the skin from her face, the way poor Pit had been flayed when the elevator exploded. If she flew that fast, she couldn't breathe. She bit her lip until it bled, clearing her mind of fear, and, more importantly, hope. She was still clinging to the tiniest fingernail ledge of optimism that she'd survive this. Exhaling, she let go, and shot off like a white-hot bullet.

As SUNDAY RACED up the tunnel, Pit ran to the computer terminal Dr. Trog had used to activate the drones. He stared at the screen, then stared at all the cables around him. His orders were to destroy everything.

But he couldn't. These computers held everything there was to know about Sunday's body. She seemed ready to die, but couldn't they just build her a new body, then swap her brain into it? It seemed like an idea from B-movie science fiction, but he was on an artificial island of talking chimps with robot servants, and the woman he loved was out doing battle with an army of headless clones. No idea sounded dumb at this point.

He tried tapping the computer keyboard. Dr. Trog had left the screen up, so he didn't need a password. The only thing Pit needed was a genius IQ and about a decade of advanced training in robotics and genetics, and making sense of what he was looking at would be a snap.

Either he hit something or Dr. Trog had planned to watch his army launch, because the screen switched to a camera shot from the top of the hospital aimed at a nearby hilltop where the army was gathered, glowing brightly. He watched as Sunday charged, and cheered as she mowed down the army with her disintegration ray. Then his voice caught in his throat as the drones fought back. He watched as, a few seconds later, the remaining drones launched like rockets, rising above the frame of the shot. Then, for reasons he couldn't guess, a half dozen of them rained back down from the sky and smashed into the burnt ground.

Without him pressing a button, the monitor went black and a scroll of white words rolled up the screen.

Tokyo: Aborted
Seoul: Aborted
Mexico City: Aborted
New York City: Active
Mumbai: Active
Jakarta: Aborted
Sao Paula: Active
Delhi: Aborted.

The list continued. Pit didn't even recognize half these cities. A handful of American cities stood out to him: Los Angeles, Chicago, Houston, San Francisco, Washington, Dallas, Detroit. All were active except for Houston and Washington.

Pit left the terminal and ran up the tunnel. He emerged beneath a darkening sky with a row of glowing stars spread out above him. An even brighter light raced up from the center of Goodall, blazing like a comet. He squinted but couldn't tell if there was a human figure at the center of the light, let alone whether or not it had a head.

All around him were severed body parts. A woman. Lot's of women, actually. Bloodied tits and asses everywhere he looked.

No heads.

Sunday wasn't part of this field of death.

He ran back toward the hospital, taking the above ground path. "Space donut!" he cried out, panting. "Space donut!

Eleven!" That was right. "Eleven!" But, there was no answer. Hope that the alien thing that was turning him into a space ship might help him lift off and chase after Sunday began to fade.

He made it into town. Robotic fire trucks were rolling down the main drag. A dozen convertibles were on fire. Burnt chimps were sprawled on the sidewalks. Pit leaned against the wall of the parking deck catching his breath.

There was a kind of a whistling sound from somewhere, followed by a thump. He lurched forward but didn't fall. He couldn't feel his legs. He looked down and found he was now pinned through his middle to the concrete wall behind him by a four-foot-long shaft of steel a quarter inch around. He looked like a bug pinned to a board.

Without warning, a shadowy form that almost looked like a man grabbed his right arm and pressed it up against the concrete wall. *Fffffip! Thump!* A second steel rod now emerged from his wrist, trapping his arm.

The shadow man punched his hand under Pit's chin and slammed his head back into the wall. *Fffffip! Thump!*

"Ow," said Pit, going cross-eyed as he tried to see what had happened. He couldn't move his head at all. His thoughts felt scrambled. Was there really a long steel rod jutting out of the top of his forehead?

His eyes focused on a woman floating in the air a hundred feet away. Skyrider? She was holding an enormous rifle. She squeezed the trigger and suddenly he couldn't move his other hand.

"God!" the woman shouted. "This job is so much easier when you have the right tools!"

"End Shadow Mode," said a voice he'd heard before. He could just see the top of Ap's head.

"Pit Geek, the vessel known as Pangea has just entered American waters. We've been authorized by the proper authorities to seize this ship."

"Ship?" Pit was confused. "This is an island! And the Chinese are gonna go to war to defend it!"

"Even the Chinese will recognize our rights to defend our

borders from trespassing vessels. Pangea's made of plastic and it floats. It has anchors. I believe that any court of law will accept the argument that this place is little more than an oversized garbage barge. Everyone on board will be taken into custody until the finer legal matters have been resolved. You will be treated a little differently, however. For the crimes you've committed against humanity, you're under arrest. You have a right to remain silent."

"I'll talk," Pit said, firmly. "You listen. A couple of dozen copies of Sunday just rocketed out of here like bats out of hell and are going to explode over the most populated cities on earth. A couple of hundred million people are gonna die if you don't stop them."

"Sundancer is next on our agenda," said Skyrider, floating closer.

"No, dammit!" Pit shouted. "Sunday ain't the problem. Dr. Trog has sent a whole army of copies out to wipe out humankind. Stop them first! I can show you where to find a list of their targets!"

Skyrider looked at the stars. The Sundancer legion was now very far off. "I wondered what all those lights were," she mumbled. Then she turned to Ap. "I'm going to give chase."

"They're pretty far away," said Ap.

Skyrider nodded and said, "Simpson, can you cut and paste me about twenty miles due west and about a mile straight up? I need to catch up to some fleeing suspects."

Suddenly, she was gone.

"Double-density mode," said Ap. He yanked free the steel rod holding Pit's head to the wall.

"Christ almighty, that smarts," said Pit, squeezing his eyes shut.

"You're going to show me the list of targets," said Ap. "These rods are coated in nanite tracers. Simpson can now fix on their signal and grab you with the space machine any time he wants. Fuck with me, and he'll drop you inside a volcano. We clear?"

"Clear," said Pit, rubbing his wrists as Ap freed his arms. "I won't be no trouble. I need . . . I need your help. Sunday's dying. Dr. Trog said he'd used your belt technology to make the copies of Sunday. You're supposed to be a hero. Save her! Make her a new body!"

"Hold on," said Ap. "I'm not following you at all. Who's Dr. Trog? What does my belt have to do with anything?"

Pit explained it as best he could as they ran back to the tunnel. Ap nearly tripped and fell when Pit said the name Code4U.

"She was a chimp?" he screamed, recovering his footing to keep up. He shook his head. "Man, you can't trust anyone in a chat room."

Back in the basement, Ap whistled as he looked around the room. "You know, it's been something of a mystery why used game systems cost so much these days. I think I just figured out where all the old boxes are going to."

"These are just old game boxes?" Pit asked.

"I'm sure they've been modified," said Ap. "But they're nothing to sneeze at. The graphic card on one of these has more computing power than was available to NASA when they put men on the moon. String together a couple of thousand like this, and you can crunch some serious numbers."

Ap plopped down in front of the system. Enough time had elapsed for the screen to go blank. As he tapped the keys, it asked for a password.

"Try 'banana,'" said Pit.

"That's racist," said Ap. But he gave it a shot anyway.

"Ha," said Pit as the screen returned to the list of cities.

"Simpson!" said Ap. "I just activated my retinal camera. You've got a list of a dozen cities in front of you that are being targeted for destruction by individuals who have the same powers as Sundancer. Like her, they're small enough and fly low enough that most traditional defenses won't spot them. We need jets in the air defending every target ASAP!"

Pit couldn't hear Simpson answer, but Ap gave a nod that looked as if he'd just gotten confirmation of his orders.

Pit said, "There were more than a dozen."

Ap said, "Well, now there's only eleven. Skyrider doesn't mess around on this saving the world stuff. She's been doing it a long time."

"So have me and Sunday," said Pit. "Except. You know. On the opposite side."

She hasn't moved since I got here. She just hangs there, a little sliver of the sun, shining down on us goats and chickens and fools.

Used to think that one bullet was for her. But, I'm starving. So thirsty I've drank my own pee. I've been here so long even my pubes have turned white. I bet I'm a hundred years old. Hell, maybe older.

Nothing rots here, but I age. I age because I'm human.

And so was she.

And she's dead. Starved or died of thirst, or maybe her air burned up. She went all alone, a long, long time ago.

The revolver is cold and heavy in my hands.

Typing out these little scraps of memory used to keep me from blowing my brains out. We all want our stories told.

But my story has come to an end.

Chapter Sixteen
Burn Baby Burn

SUNDAY'S CLEAVER had long since melted. Her arms ached. Her hands were numb. She had trouble feeling the ceramic knife in her grasp.

She wasn't keeping count. She wasn't even thinking now. She was flying faster than she'd ever flown, far too fast to think, outracing sound in utter, eerie silence, all the whispers of doubt long since left behind.

She climbed back toward the stratosphere. She wasn't sure how she was still breathing. The shock wave of compressed air that had formed when she'd gone supersonic had spared her from her most morbid visions of wind ripping off her flesh. The high-pressure air seemed trapped even when she pushed up to the very edge of space to find her next target. They were getting harder and harder to spot, both because they were fewer in number and because they were now back in daylight.

There.

She dove, pushing to speeds she couldn't even estimate. Mach six? Mach seven? Mach eight? Photons were flying out of her at the speed of light. Was there any limit to her speed beyond the one Einstein had written down?

She slowed as she raced up behind her target. She readied her knife and went in for the kill.

At the last second, the drone spun and pushed Sunday's arm away. A few of the other drones had spotted her and shown similar rudimentary defenses, but she'd fought those before her arms turned to lead.

The drone kneed her in the belly and they both went into a tailspin. The drone kept her hands clamped on Sunday's knife hand.

If this was the last one, it didn't matter if they both plunged into the ocean. If it wasn't . . .

She eyed the camera cluster where the head should be. Why didn't these things burn? The chimps were geniuses, and were developing a reputation for building advanced materials that were stronger, lighter, and tougher than anything humans had whipped up. But, this was still just matter. Even if the Sundancer body was immune to solar radiation, this thing had to have a melting point.

She set out to find it. The ceramic knife suddenly warped like a vinyl record, then vanished in a spray of droplets. She felt the old pressure building in her gut as they raced toward the ocean and with a sudden release the wormholes surrounding her doubled, then tripled. The webcam vaporized and the drone went limp.

Sunday never reached the surface of the ocean, because the surface of the ocean moved as she approached it, boiling away in a flash. She pulled from her spin and climbed.

She tried to close the wormholes, to reduce her intensity.

She couldn't find the invisible switch in her mind that controlled them.

With so much power channeling out of her, the second she switched off, she was going to die.

And she didn't want to die.

A blue blur flashed across the corner of her vision. It was Skyrider, racing toward her much faster than the drones had moved. She was carrying a ridiculously large rifle, which she aimed at Sunday. She pulled the trigger when she was only a few hundred feet away.

Whatever came out of the barrel vaporized when it came within a dozen feet of Sunday. Skyrider veered to avoid a collision, but passed close enough that her rifle turned to putty in her hands. Suddenly, her flight suit caught fire, including her helmet.

Skyrider slid to a hover and yanked her helmet off, gasping for breath. Her face was covered in silver mesh. As the flaming fragments of her suit fell away, the silver mesh proved to cover her whole body, even her face, sheer as pantyhose.

Skyrider squinted as she stared at Sunday. "You've got a head!"

"I'm the original," Sunday shouted back.

"There are only three left," Skyrider shouted. "But we've got radar locks on all of them and missiles in the air. Time to draw the curtain on your little doomsday play!"

"I didn't want this!" Sunday screamed. "I tried to stop it!"

"Then stand down," said Skyrider. "Turn off your flames and surrender."

"I can't!" she screamed. "I think . . . Dr. Trog pumped the drones full of adrenaline so that they would be living bombs. I'm running on nothing but adrenaline now!" She swallowed hard. "I think . . . I think I'm going to explode."

Skyrider said, "You don't have to explode! Just turn down your flame and wait. The Covenant employs the finest scientific minds on the planet. We can fix this!"

"Call them!" screamed Sunday. "I surrender! Just do what you can to save me before I take half the planet with me."

"Um," said Skyrider. "I can't call them, actually. My radio was in my helmet."

"I don't have time to wait for you to get help!" said Sunday. She looked down at the glimmering blue ocean. She saw a few patches of white sand in the distance. "Where are we?" she asked.

"Just north of Midway atoll," Skyrider shouted. "The island is empty except for a research station. Don't move! I'll go use their radio to call Covenant Command."

PIT COULDN'T BELIEVE what he was hearing. Ap was still pumping his fists in the air.

"We've won?" he asked.

"Servant ambushed a drone over Nevada and Chinese jets just shot down the last one!"

"I thought Servant was dragging the island?"

"How could you know that?"

"Dr. Trog told us."

Ap shrugged. "We Covenant move in mysterious ways."

"Right," said Pit. "Space machine." He rubbed the hole in the back of his skull. "I probably would have got that if you hadn't just pulled a damned metal spike out of my brains. Anyway, if the drones are finished, what happened to Sunday?"

"Not sure," said Ap. "Skyrider had visual contact, but then we lost her signal."

Pit shook his head. "Sunday fried her."

"Don't think so. The lab boys have outfitted her with some fancy thermal underwear."

"What have long-johns got to do with anything?"

"Not that kind of thermal underwear," said Ap. "It's a silver mesh networked into the space machine. It detects highly energized particles that collide with it and automatically cuts and pastes them into the earth's core. Sundancer can blast all she wants but Sarah won't even get a tan." Suddenly, Ap stiffened, and sat up straighter in his chair. "Hold on. I'm getting a message from Simpson." He grabbed Pit by the wrist. "You wouldn't be a World War Two buff by any chance?"

"I spent most of the war years drunk," said Pit.

"Too bad," said Ap. "We're about to be tourists at one of the most iconic sites in the Pacific!"

Then Pit experienced the familiar sensation of being folded by the space machine. The backs of his elbows twisted to slide along under his nuts as his eyeballs bent to stare directly at one another. Then he dropped to his knees on a beach of white sand.

Ap was by his side, and Servant and Skyrider were standing in front of him. It was high noon, with the sun directly overhead. Except, as he looked to the west, the sun was also down on the horizon.

"What's he doing here," Servant growled, staring at Pit.

"You want me to just leave him?" asked Ap.

"I want him in a cell!"

"He's eaten himself out of every jail he's ever been thrown into," said Skyrider. "He's probably safer in our custody." Pit tried not to stare, but he could see all of Skyrider's lady parts through the mesh of her thermal underwear.

"Here's the situation," said Skyrider. "Sundancer says she feels like she's about to explode. She's putting out enough radiation that if she were over a population center right now, people would already be dying. I've already had Simpson cut and paste the researchers here to safety, but safety isn't what it used to be. If she experiences the sort of exponential flare up we witnessed in some of the aborted drones, she could carve a hole out of the planet that would rival the comet impact that killed off the dinosaurs. Nowhere is safe."

"Cut and paste her out into space," said Ap.

Skyrider shook her head. "We never got any targeting nanites into her. And, with the radiation she's putting out, satellite sensors just go blind when we try to get a lock."

Servant shook his head. "Is this a joke? Let's just break her neck."

"The problem with that—" Skyrider never finished her sentence.

"Up one mile, Simpson," said Servant. He vanished.

They all stared at one another, wondering what to do next.

Suddenly the sun overhead began to fall toward them.

"Ghost mode!" shouted Ap.

Sand and seashells flew all around them as Sunday and Servant slammed into the island half a mile away.

"Breaking her neck might trigger the explosion!" Skyrider shouted.

"Servant!" Ap screamed. "Stand down! Stand down!"

A volcano began erupting where the two had crashed. Beads of flaming lava rained down, sizzling as they burned little holes into Pit's clothes and the flesh beneath.

"He's not answering!" Ap said, sounding panicked.

The heat and light pouring of the spit of land were almost unbearable. Even here, the sea was boiling. Hurricane force winds hotter than a furnace nearly knocked Pit from his feet.

Pit lunged at Skyrider and grabbed her by the shoulders. "Strip!" he said.

"Excuse me?" she asked.

"Take off that fancy underwear! I need it. I'm the only one who can stop her!"

"Johnny, if you record a single frame of this I will murder you," she said, eying Ap.

"You're going to do it?" Ap asked.

"I don't have a better idea!" she said, lowering the invisible nanozipper that sealed the front. Pit averted his eyes. It was what a good cowboy would do. She shoved the suit into his hands and said, "Ap, I can't stay here without protection. You're safe in ghost mode. It's up to the two of you!"

Ap nodded.

Then, she was gone.

Pit struggled to pull on the flimsy garment. He didn't know what the hell it was made of, but it was tough. Real panty hose would have ripped as he pulled them on over his jagged toenails. Not that he'd ever tried that, mind you. The springy fabric stretched over his clothes, but he felt like his balls were being pushed up into his belly as he tried to yank the suit tight and pull the hood over his head. When he finally had it on, Ap pointed out the zipper, which Pit would never have found on his own.

"I'm coming with you," said Ap.

They marched into the inferno across bubbling earth, along shores now completely dry as the ocean was pushed back a mile in every direction. Once or twice Pit fell, and had to crawl in the face of the horrible winds. Even protected from the heat, his mouth and nose and eyes went completely dry in air where every molecule of water had been torn asunder.

They reached the crater where Servant and Sunday had fallen. It was now a sheet of glass. In the center a giant man was sprawled, covered in third degree burns. He wasn't moving. The flesh was half gone from his monstrous face.

"Servant!" Ap cried out as he ran toward his fallen comrade. He knelt and placed a hand on the big man's chest.

"He dead?" Pit asked.

"I don't know," said Ap. "I think he's breathing, but

apparently his invulnerability had limits." He grimaced. "The radiation here is killing all radio signals. I can't get Simpson to grab him."

Ap stood, and they kept walking into the blast furnace wind.

Further down the beach was Sunday. She sat with her knees drawn up to her chest, her arms wrapped around them, staring at the sunset.

Pit slogged through magma to reach her. He placed his hand on her shoulder.

She looked up. "Is there hope?" she asked.

Her eyes had already answered the question.

He dropped to his knees and wrapped his arm around her. She rubbed her cheek against his cheek. They kissed once again. Her lips were completely dry.

"I can't stop burning," she whispered.

"Then don't," he said, his voice trembling. "Just . . . do what you do best. Burn, baby. Burn."

And then he opened his other mouth and closed his eyes. There was a familiar tickle at the back of his throat, and a burning sensation that lasted a long time. When he opened his eyes she was gone.

Ap stumbled as the hurricane force wind suddenly died. "What just happened?" he stared at the bubbling sand where she'd just sat. "Did . . . did she just get away?"

"Naw," said Pit, his voice barely audible. There was a pit in the center of his chest where all his breath felt trapped.

"Is . . . is the world safe?" Ap asked, scratching his hair, or trying to. In his ghost mode, itches apparently were impossible to relieve.

"Naw," said Pit, swallowing hard. "No more than it ever was. Nobody ever gets out of here alive."

"Let me get Simpson online," said Ap. "Time to go home. Well, my home, at least. Guess you're going to have a new home."

"Yeah," said Pit. "Guess I will." Then he shoved his fist into his mouth. He swallowed. And kept swallowing.

PIT ARRIVED in a world of trash. The place was a vast ring he couldn't begin to measure, in orbit around an elongated star that poured out heat and light. He'd pulled off the thermal underwear and shouted at her for days, or what felt like days. There was no way to measure time. She never showed any signs of hearing him.

There wasn't much gravity. Things in the ring did tend to pull together, though. Hungry for the first time in memory, he'd found an intact jar of pickled eggs in the garbage. He was certain he'd die of the thirst their vinegar saltiness left in his mouth until he found an old soda machine and managed to pry it open with a crowbar he'd swallowed back in 1973. For a long, immeasurable time, he drank sodas and ate from a desiccated deer carcass while he watched living chickens and goats cavorting in the distance.

He'd started needing to pee after about his third soda, and had to take a crap not too long after that, wiping himself with pages from a Dallas phone book. It wasn't his first clue, but it felt like proof that he was normal again. Whatever Eleven had done to freeze his body in time no longer had any effect on him.

One day he found a typewriter. An old one, a Remington, completely manual. Just like the one he'd written his screenplay on. To keep from going crazy, he'd started typing, filling up scrap paper and bits of card and anything flat he could roll through the machine. When the letters had finally faded to nothingness, he thinned out ink from a ballpoint pen using his own urine and soaked the ribbon to refresh it. He was surprised when this actually worked.

He was always worried that one day he would run out of paper. But, in the end, he ran out of memories. He ran out of things to say.

So he'd placed a pistol against the roof of his mouth.

And then, for a time, he'd been dead.

IT WAS NIGHTTIME when he woke up. He was stretched out on short, thick green grass, like what you'd find on a golf course. He sat up and saw a glimmering sea in the distance.

He could tell from the air that he was back on Pangea. Eleven floated before him.

"I've completed my mission. It's time for us to leave."

"Oh," said Pit. "What mission was that?"

"I came here to catalogue the sentient beings of this planet. I've finished my recording of the beings of this world, as well as the five sentients from this planet that currently reside on Mars."

"There are men on Mars?"

"You've met two of them," said Eleven. "As for their offspring, I'm unsure you would classify them as men."

Pit looked at his hands. They were young and strong again. Well, not young. He looked like he had when he was in his forties or fifties."

"Was I dead?" he asked.

"You had regressed to your lowest biological threshold," said Eleven. "Only the bacteria in your gut were still active."

"Do they count as part of me?"

"Who else would they be part of?"

Pit looked up at he stars. "You left me in there for a long time."

"In the relative time frame of your four dimensional existence, you were only gone two weeks. I saw no need to retrieve you prematurely."

"Two weeks? It felt like decades."

"Then subjectively it was," said Eleven. "There is no precise formula for reconciling times between the two realities."

Pit stood. It was then he realized he was naked. "You couldn't pull me out some clothes?"

"They will serve no purpose where we're going. If there are sentient beings in the Centauri system, it is highly unlikely they will care if you are wearing pants."

"How are we getting there?" he asked.

"We shall walk," said Eleven. "But I know a short cut." Then Eleven splintered apart and splashed against Pit's chest. Pit looked down and found himself covered with triangular stripes, like a tiger.

"Ready?" Eleven asked.

"No," said Pit. "I can't leave without . . . without knowing what happened to Sunday."

"She perished," said Eleven. "She lost the last of her control and exploded after you swallowed her. Enough solar material flowed through her wormholes that she became massive enough to organize the detritus in the zero space into an orbiting ring. This took many, many years. Due to the time variance, though you followed her inside by only seconds, she had been there for decades. If the channeling of solar mass failed to kill her, by the time you arrived she had long since failed to receive the primitive but necessary chemical fuels that powered her life functions."

Pit closed his eyes and breathed slowly. He'd had a long time to accept the reality that Sunday had died. What had he expected to feel now that it was confirmed? He missed her just as much as ever.

"You fixed me," he whispered, holding up his hand. He opened his eyes, staring at the stripes that now coated it. "Fix her."

"We're a braided life-form," said Eleven. "I can restore your cognitive abilities because your thoughts are my thoughts. Even if I could reassemble Sunday's material form, she would not be the person you knew. For now, her presence within our dimensional hold is most fortuitous. The solar radiation she emits will provide plentiful power for our travels. Were it not for her, you would need to devour a mass the size of Mount Everest to generate the required energy for us to escape this planet."

Pit nodded. He crossed his arms across his chest.

It wasn't fair, but that wasn't the way of the world. Some travelers reached the end of their journeys while those who loved them traveled on. Like every other person, all he could take were memories, and the warmth of knowing that he would always carry some part of her inside him.

Only, less metaphorically.

He stepped forward, and was gone from earth.

On a world with green skies he gawked at unfamiliar stars. Despite his grief, he tilted back his head and laughed, so hard he had to wipe tears from his eyes.

He'd gotten out alive.

Also by James Maxey

Nobody Gets the Girl

The Dragon Age Trilogy
Bitterwood
Dragonforge
Dragonseed

The Dragon Apocalypse Series
Greatshadow
Hush
Witchbreaker
Soulless

There is No Wheel (Short Story Collection)

If you've enjoyed Burn Baby Burn, let the world know with a review on Amazon, Goodreads, or similar sites. Reviews are the lifeblood of independent fiction. Thank you!
--James Maxey

About the Author

James Maxey lives in Hillsborough, NC with his wife Cheryl and a clowder of unruly cats. A lifetime of reading comic books has diminished his mental capacity to the point that he spends all his waking moments trapped in violent daydreams about colorfully clad superhumans and large man-eating, fire-breathing reptiles. Unsuited for productive work or the company of decent people, James ekes out a living by punching the keys of a steam-powered typewriter at random day in, day out. Occasionally, these meaningless streams of letters arrange themselves into something resembling stories, which he fleeces without remorse to the depraved subset of humanity known as 'readers.' If you are the sort of person who can't help but stare at car crashes, you can read more about James by visiting his blog at dragonprophet.blogspot.com.

CPSIA information can be obtained at www.ICGtesting.com
Printed in the USA
LVOW07s2231170913

352935LV00011B/189/P